Brandy

Happy Reading!

Willow: *June*
Mystic Zodiac
Book 6

Brandy Walker

1

QUOTE:

Of only casting a spell on a man was as simple as it sounded. Not to fall in love...but to send him hurling off the edge of the Earth.

~ Willow

BLURB:

She's a witch looking for the love of her life…

Willow Davies is pinning all of her hopes on the Summer Solstice Celebration. She calls to the Goddess Aphrodite in the light of the moon to help find the love of her life, the man who is meant to complete her heart and soul, and Aphrodite answers. But Aphrodite warns that love can be surprising and by the Gods she meant it.

He's the warlock she's always seen as her nemesis…

Cedric Stone is ready to claim Willow as the love of his life, except she still considers him the enemy. They've known each other all of their lives and after a blind date gone horribly wrong, thanks to him, he realizes he's in love with her. It's his good fortune when he shows up on her doorstep and sees her wearing an enchanted moonstone, a gem known to be worn by those looking for love. It's the perfect way into her life.

What happens when he becomes the one she can't live without?

As the days go by and they spend more and more time together, Willow begins to wonder how much of Cedric's attention is because he truly is in love with her or because she's wearing an enchanted moonstone.

PROLOGUE

Eros sent the panicked young maiden away to answer the door; after she came scurrying into his room with news someone was approaching. Visitors were not expected at such an ungodly hour. The shades were still drawn, and he lounged in bed contemplating what to do to his sweet Chloe when he saw her again. All rendezvous had come to a halt after the bet began; yet, he wondered if that had been such a good idea. Chloe didn't seem as inclined to curb her lusty nature.

He knew she had seen the Great Watcher again, though not the extent of their time together. The handmaiden he had bribed to spy on her came back with news that Gabriel had been at Chloe's home. She saw him lounging outside, as if waiting for something or someone.

Eros knew he would have to find a way to loosen Chloe's luscious lips. Possibly with heated kisses and nibbles of her soft skin. He would arouse and seduce to get the information he wanted.

The girl scurried back into his room with the object of his obsession hot on her heels.

"I do not need you to announce me, girl. Leave us."

The girl's eyes widened, and he could see fear and indecision warring in them.

"Go," he said, and the girl practically ran from the room. He placed his hands behind his head, ensuring the sheet slipped down, showing off his chest when he moved. "You can't go around scaring off all my help, Chloe. Who would take care of me then?" He pouted, sticking his lower lip out.

She rolled her eyes and planted her hands on her hips, thrusting her chest, those glorious breasts toward him. "I imagine you could find some *other* young maiden willing to wait on you hand and foot. As a matter of fact, I may have a handmaiden ripe for the job, seeing as she will no longer be in *my* household."

Damn. Eros worked to keep his disappointment at his spy being found out from his face. "Oh dear, what happened? Did she make a play for your Great Watcher?" *Double damn.* This time he grimaced when he saw the look of victory on Chloe's face. Well, he would wipe that smirk right off.

He flung the covers off and stood, showing off every

8

inch of his six foot six, well-endowed frame.

Chloe's gaze dropped straight to his straining erection, a by-product of thinking of her, and her expressive brown eye's grew huge. Her mouth opened on a hitched breath, and he had a moment's pride fill his chest.

"You," she said with a harsh whisper.

"Me," he said and smirked. Her nipples pebbled against the soft fabric of her chiton, pushing against it, calling to him. He knew exactly what he wanted to do to punish her for seeing another man.

"I was going to give you an easy couple this month, mainly because things got a little — out of hand in May." He waited for her to argue that they hadn't, but she didn't respond.

"Chloe?"

"Hmmm," she hummed, eyes still riveted below his waist.

"Eyes up here."

Her glazed gaze lifted to his and he smiled. It did wonders to his slightly bruised pride to see her so enamored. He may not have liked her calling him a hot piece of ass, but he knew when to use it to his advantage.

He moved forward and into her body in a bid to help her concentrate. Too bad he didn't think it all the way through. The unbelievably soft linen of her gown brushed against his heated skin; sending a shiver down his spine. He wrapped an arm around her waist, unable to resist.

He cleared his throat, it coming out more pained than anything. "As I was saying."

"Yes," she said, her voice husky. "As you were saying."

"I planned to give you an easier couple. One destined to meet."

Her forehead furrowed slightly. There was the argument he had been waiting for.

He cut her off before she could start, though. Much longer pressed up against her body, and he might end up taking her to bed, nullifying the bet altogether. It sounded fantastic to his cock, but he wanted more. He wanted to see her win. To see the triumph glimmering in her dark eyes. "But, since you did such a wonderful job, I thought I would give you a real challenge."

He pressed his lips to hers quickly. "For the month of the witch, I will give you one who worships many Gods and Goddesses, to include my mother. Willow's intended is the bane of her existence, Cedric Stone. A warlock who could be even more promiscuous than me."

Chloe licked her lips, and he knew she was gathering his taste. "Impossible," she said. "No one is as wanton as you."

Eros slid his hand down her back to cup her buttocks. He pulled her as close as he could, and ground his erection into her stomach. "Is that your way of saying you want to
10

find out? Right." He kissed her. "This." He kissed her again, but lingered a little longer. "Second." His last kiss had him sinking into the warm depths of her mouth. Their tongues tangled and when he found he needed air to breathe, he pulled away and nipped her bottom lip.

Chloe's fingers went to her lip, and her eyes flared with banked heat. "Oh my," she whispered before turning and fleeing.

Eros chuckled at her retreating figure. That surely had to remind her of what she wanted, what she needed from him. He fell back onto his bed and took his cock in his hand. Bringing himself to orgasm with the remembered feel of her body pressed against his.

CHAPTER ONE

Jun 1ˢᵗ – Monday

Willow looked around her backyard and wondered, for the millionth time, if what she was about to do was actually a good idea…or not. It was the middle of the night, and she stood under the waxing moon in nothing but a thin, sheer red robe about to invoke the Goddess Aphrodite to help her in her plight.

If she intended to find the love of her life, she needed the help of a much higher power. Nothing she'd done over the last several years had worked. Going to bars. Hitting the clubs. Finding men at solstice celebrations or coven gatherings. She'd even gone the blind date route, allowing family and friends to set her up. The only things she had gained from the experience were how to deal with disappointment and rejection. The men, family and friends had set her up with, were complete duds.

One guy she'd gone on a blind date with asked her where she'd parked her broom, and just ten minutes *after* they sat down and their food was ordered. It was one stereotypical quip after another from him. She left midway through dinner, having had enough, and went home to cleanse her aura.

Another date asked her to chain him up and treat him like a sexual sacrifice. She'd called her cousin Autumn, as she sat across from him, and told her she'd found the man of *her* dreams. Autumn rushed over and snatched him up. They were married a week later.

The most recent disaster happened a couple of weeks ago, and involved a shifter whose name she couldn't even remember. She met him for lunch and was promptly told he wasn't interested in her, would never date someone like her, but *would* love her help finding his mate. With each painful word the shifter spouted, she turned a deeper shade of red; her embarrassment skyrocketing until she wanted to slide under the table and pray no one found her...ever.

She discovered that her childhood nemesis, Cedric, had told the man she could cast a locator spell to find his destined mate. She could, but she wouldn't. Why reward a man when he could have come to her directly and asked, instead of feigning interest in her?

Knowing Cedric was behind the faux date explained his appearance seconds after she stepped through the door of the café, and why he watched the entire uncomfortable episode. She was a pawn for his amusement, once again.

It really was a pity she couldn't have hexed the bastard

when the shifter told her Cedric was the one who told him to ask her out. But witches were forbidden from using spells on Witch and Warlock kind. Not that it didn't happen, though. In fact, it occurred a lot more than a person would think. She just preferred to play by the rules.

And maybe that was her problem, she thought as she breathed in the crisp cool evening air.

Willow set four white candles around the stone bowl she had filled with water earlier. Her precious pale blue moonstone wrapped in copper soaked in it. The threads of moonlight seeped into the stone, charging it with the moon's power. After the invocation and calling, she would attach her precious gem to the copper chainmail necklace made especially for it. The two items a gateway for the blessing she craved.

They were her last ditch efforts to attract her one true love. To find the man who would complete her soul and ease the yearning deep inside. She was sick of being alone and watching everyone else fall in love. In the grand scheme of problems, not having a love life, or someone to call her own, wasn't much of one. But her heart ached, and loneliness was a bitch.

Even her good friend Celeste had found a man that complimented her perfectly. A wood elf that possessed a love of nature and animals that rivaled Celeste's, who lavished her with the love and affection she dreamt about.

Willow had heard he'd recently moved in with Celeste. Choosing to trek into the forest to watch over the animals during the week, fulfilling his obligation to them. On the weekends, they would hole up in his cabin nestled deep in the woods. Goddess knew what they filled their days and nights with out there.

You know what they're doing, and you're jealous. Why else would you be out here charging your moonstone, set on wearing it day and night through the Summer Solstice?

If nothing happened by the setting of the 21st, she would give up her dream and commit to a life alone. At nearly twenty-eight, it was probably past time by witch standards.

Enough! She admonished herself. It was time to begin the rite. She let out a huge breath and cleared her mind of everything but Aphrodite and her truest wish. She slid her thumb from the fingertips of her pointer and index fingers down to the second knuckle, murmuring *ignis* to produce a flame from the tips. It was almost like clicking the button on a lighter. She started her invocation.

In the name of Aphrodite, (She lit the first candle)
Goddess of love, (She lit the second candle)
Beauty, (She lit the third candle)
And Fertility, (She lit the last candle)
I invoke thee. (She flicked her fingers and the flame went out)
Bless this stone and all it represents.
Help it bring to me my one true desire.
The love of my life.
The light of my soul.
The man who completes me,
Makes me whole.
In the name of Aphrodite,
Goddess of love, (She blew out the first candle, going in the opposite direction)
16

Beauty, (She blew out the second candle)
And fertility, (She blew out the third candle)
As I will it, it shall be so! (She blew out the final candle)

She closed the rite and thanked the Goddess for her
time. Plucking the stone from the moon water, she held it
in her hands. Warmth spread through her palms and up
her arms. It seeped into her chest, locking her breath in her
lungs. Her hands began to glow, illuminated by the stone
within, turning the warmth into a raging heat coursing
through her blood.

The urge to scream was hampered by a lack of air, and
only when she felt she would pass out did her lungs begin to
work again. She inhaled, then let it out like a set of bellows,
the long stream of air focused until there was nothing left.
Her chest felt compressed and she got lightheaded. In
the fog of tying to get normal function from her body, a
woman's voice whispered in her ear.

"Willow, my child, you gift me with your servitude and
I shall repay it. Wear your stone, and you will find what you
want. But take heed, love can be surprising." There was a
soft press of lips against her forehead for a second before the
phantom woman disappeared.

The heat of the stone in her hands dissipated, and when
she opened them up, the moonstone held a soft glow. She
hoped it meant good things were to come.

CHAPTER TWO

Jun 2nd – Tuesday

Willow was pulled away from the numerous coven proposals spread out over her kitchen table, and the monthly calendar she was trying to fill, by a knock at her front door. She glanced at the huge clock on the wall, and saw it was a little after nine in the morning.

She frowned. "I wonder who that could be?" She asked her cat Edward, who was curled up on a set of papers she'd given up hope of going over at the moment. Edward flicked his tail lazily and yawned before closing his dark eyes.

"Of course, you don't care. Must not be someone you want to suck magic from." She stood and went to answer the front door. Thankfully, whoever it was wasn't in a hurry. They didn't knock repeatedly, impatient for her to get there. Sometimes her visitors could be dicks if she wasn't there after the first rap on the wood.

She squinted, looking through the peephole. Whoever had been there clearly wasn't anymore. She shrugged and turned to head back into the kitchen when there was another knock.

Not bothering to check to see who it was, in the hopes of catching them, she unbolted the lock and swung open the door. She poked her head out, as she didn't see anyone on the porch. A look to the left revealed the source of the disturbance, and her day went from promising to shit in a matter of seconds.

Cedric Stone, the man who lived to annoy her, leaned his fine ass against the end of the porch railing, a lazy smile on his face. Mischief danced in his forest green eyes, and she knew just by looking at him, she wasn't going to like whatever reason he had for being on her front porch so early in the morning. In reality, he should still be in bed with whichever bimbo, or bimbos, he was romancing at the moment. They fell at his feet like trees during deforestation. They were about as smart too. Even when he tossed them aside for someone new after a week or two, they clung to the hope he would allow them back into his life.

She fervently hoped Cedric wasn't the Goddess's answer to Willow's desire. If so, then she wanted her money back. Willow just didn't get what was so amazing about him.

The tiny voice in the back of her head laughed hysterically at the lie she told herself, and anyone else if they bothered asking.

Okay, so the man looked like a Greek God with his chiseled features, hard-packed muscles and crazy tousled, just rolled out of bed hair.

As if knowing the direction of her thoughts, he pushed his fingers through the thick mane and smirked.

Willow frowned at the direction of her thoughts, and shook her head to clear them. She was still pissed at him for that debacle of a date he had set her up with. Could it really be called a date when the guy clearly had no interest in her? "What do you want?"

"Ah, Wills, is that any way to greet the man of your dreams?"

"For the millionth time, stop calling me Wills," she said, frustration edging her voice. He had been calling her that ever since they started elementary school together. He had said she looked like a boy and should have a boy's name. The rest of his little cronies laughed and followed his lead. At the age of five, Cedric already possessed a commanding personality that sucked people in by the hordes.

Damn warlock! She took a quick breath. "And for the record, you are *not* the man of my dreams, so get that idiotic thought out of your head right this minute!"

"I think you're lying. I see the way you look at me. Those coy smiles and heated stares."

She pressed her lips together in annoyance. She knew his game. He would take anything she said to the contrary, and spin it to sound like she was desperate for him. "No, it's more like I want you to fall off the edge of the earth. That is a bit of a dream of mine when it comes to you. In that regard, you might be right."

"You wound me," he said, pressing his hand to his heart. He pushed away from the railing and came toward her. He had one of those loose-hipped swaggers that drew attention, which had women drooling while imagining how damn good he would be in bed. And, she had heard from multiple sources...he was *really* good. Like off the charts, ruined-a-woman-for-any-other-man good.

Damn it! She didn't want him in bed. She didn't want to know how much of a sex god he was. She wanted him gone.

Off her porch.

Off her property.

Out of her life.

Liar!

She crossed her arms and stood her ground, intent on keeping him out of her house. She had cleansed it with sage not even a month ago after his last visit; she didn't feel like doing it again so soon. Not when she had other things to worry about and occupy her time.

The Summer Solstice celebrations started in less than two weeks, and there was a ton of work to do. Like the previous year, she volunteered to help out. She knew which permits were needed. Had obtained the contacts with the fire department already. Knew the best way to wrangle newbie

22

witches who had recently upgraded from their learner's permits—a keeper, they always needed a keeper.

Dealing with Cedric and whatever inane request he had wasn't going to happen. Not this time. She didn't have the patience for it. And she was finally…*finally* putting her foot down. He stressed her out on a normal day; during the Summer Solstice celebrations, she'd go gray prematurely and probably a lot batty.

He stopped in front of her, forcing her to look at up him. She cursed her shorter stature that allowed him to tower over her. He was almost a full foot taller than her five foot six frame, and it pissed her off. Gah! Everything about him pissed her off.

Keep telling yourself that girlie, the little voice in the back of her head taunted.

Willow ground her teeth together. "I doubt the wound is deep. Tell me what you need so I can tell you no and you can leave. I have a lot to do today and no time for whatever foolishness you have in mind. And no, I will not teach any more of your dippy girlfriends spells. And I will not let any of your idiotic friends stay here during the celebrations because your place isn't big enough. You should have thought about that when you decided to get the apartment with your brother."

"Ah, come on, Wills. Why do you have to be such a stick in the mud?" Cedric reached out and brushed a lock of her wayward hair from her face. She jolted at the contact, and her moonstone warmed against her skin. Her hand drifted up, and she grasped it between her fingers. *Please, don't tell me it's reacting to him.* Heat flared, then it cooled within seconds. She breathed a sigh of relief. *False alarm.*

CHAPTER THREE

Cedric followed the path of her hand, and was surprised when he saw her clutch a pale blue moonstone resting against her creamy skin. Mystics, along with humans-in-the-know, that wanted to attract true love, were known to wear the stone. It was said to arouse passion, enhance fertility, as well as protect sensitive emotions. Some people even had it enchanted with a love spell, even though there was no such thing in the world. A smart Mystic knew to leave that up to Fate and the Gods and Goddesses.

So why the hell was she wearing it?

He knew the necklace and stone were new. She hadn't been wearing it when he showed up a month ago with... *damn, what was her name?* He thought for a second, but it didn't come to him. Her name didn't matter in the long run.

25

The girl had been a means to an end, something to parade in front of Willow to get a reaction. It was his bad luck that every reaction from his beautiful green-eyed witch was one of irritation.

He also hadn't seen her wearing it when he saw her a couple weeks earlier at the café during her date from hell. That had been a fiasco of great proportions, and something he regretted...a little.

He didn't know why he still antagonized her after all these years. Maybe it was born from habit stemming from their childhood. Maybe it was because he didn't know how else to get a response from her at this point in their relationship. The woman drove him nuts, and not in the crazy *I want to tear my hair out* way. No, he'd realized over the past few weeks that she drove his libido wild. Had him constantly on edge and craving her attention, especially when she held it back.

He wanted to press her on her bed, or up against a wall or door...any place he could ravish her would do, really. He hungered to feel her magic slide across him as it blended with his. Her hands caressing every inch of him. Her lips and teeth tasting and nibbling. He wanted to see her head thrown back in ecstasy, and hear his name tumble from her sweet lips like a prayer.

It wasn't all about conquering her sexually. Even though he could admit he'd wanted to do that for a *very* long time. There was more to it than that. There was a drive in the core of him pushing to be near her just for the sake of spending time with her. A basic need to get to know her without the jokes and jabs, the sneers and witty comebacks. He ached to see her smile at him genuinely. Be happy to see him.

Fuck! He wanted to be her damn friend.

"Whatcha got there?" He asked, nodding at the necklace. Needing to know the meaning behind it, and afraid of what he might hear.

She dropped the stone like it was on fire, letting it bounce off her breastbone; a cool mask fell into place on her face. The one with the dead eyes and thinned lips. He fucking *hated* that look.

"It's nothing. What do you want, Cedric?"

He reached out and took hold of the stone. It heated between his fingers, and snaps of electricity arced down them. "It doesn't feel like nothing." As a matter of fact, it felt like something pretty damned important. Something magical. Something enchanted. *Had* she put a spell on it? Was she really trying to find love?

Willow didn't need the help, regardless of what her family and friends said or thought. If she'd open her eyes, she'd see it standing right in front of her. He was ready to make her his one and only. He had a feeling she wouldn't believe him though.

It had taken him a long time to sort out how he felt about her. The day he jokingly told Reid to go out with her, then witnessed the devastation on her face when she found out why he'd asked her out, Cedric felt like he'd been hit in the head with a two-by-four. It gutted him that he was the reason for her distress. She refused to talk to him when he

27

had jogged after her. In fact, this was the first time they'd spoken since that day. She had ignored all of his phone calls and texts.

She batted his hand away and closed her hand around the stone. "What. Do. You. Want?"

"You aren't still mad at me, are you?"

"What do you think?" She glared at him, and he wondered for half a second if she was silently hexing him.

Nah, Willow would never do that. I would feel it if she did anyway. Nothing like having a magical early warning system to tip a person off. "I didn't know Reid would take me seriously about the spell thing. He never has before when I said stupid shit."

"Then why did you show up and watch the entire time with a huge smile on your face?"

Cedric grimaced and shrugged. He didn't have an answer for her. At least not one he wanted to give her. Reid told him he'd taken his advice and asked her out. As soon as the words were out of his mouth, Cedric demanded the details. He only showed up to make sure they didn't hit it off. The smile — well, at first, he'd been pleased to hear Reid say he wasn't interested in her. He had grinned like an idiot knowing he didn't have to worry about his friend flirting with her and being successful. He hadn't been smiling by the end of the faux date, though, but she probably hadn't seen. There was no way he could miss the tears shimmering in her big eyes as Reid told her he'd never be interested in a woman like her. Cedric wasn't sure what that meant, but

28

it had pissed him off enough that he'd almost sent a bolt of electricity through the guy that would trigger his shift. It would have been comical to see the guy bust out of his clothes and turn into a bear right there.

"Of course, you don't have an answer. I don't know why I bother giving you the time of day. You've caused me nothing but grief and heartache since the age of five."

"Come on, Wills. It hasn't been all bad." At least he didn't think so. "I've always thought of us as great friends." He liked it when they bantered back and forth. She was one of the few women who didn't simper and fall at his feet. *Now, if she wanted to fall to her knees…*he had to stop that thought before it finished. He wasn't here to seduce. He was there to get back into her life and good graces. A week without talking to her or hearing from her wasn't too horrible, but a couple…well that was simply too long.

"Really? I don't know how you remember our history, but there hasn't been one good moment with you — *ever*. As for being friends, I would hate to see how you treat your enemies. Now please, tell me why you're here. It certainly wasn't to apologize."

He thrust his hands into his front pockets and suppressed the urge to argue. He should tell her he was sorry, but without that eye-opening moment, he wouldn't have realized he was crazy in love with her. "I thought I would check in with my partner."

Her eyes widened and her mouth dropped open. "Partner? For what?"

"To help out with whatever it is you're doing for the upcoming celebration. The coven felt it would be best if we worked together to ensure the event went off without a hitch."

"I know how the coven feels. I was at the monthly gathering when it was decided, which is more than I can say for you. I haven't seen you at one in months." She paused and took a breath. "But, I'm getting off track. I already have a partner. Not that I need one or he's been much help." She mumbled the last part, her disgruntlement easy to hear.

"No, you have a *new* one. Perry was called out of town, and I'm his replacement."

Her dark eyes narrowed with suspicion. "Did someone con you into it? Tell you it would get you laid or something equally juvenile?"

If the Gods are on my side, yes! Cedric knew enough not to say that out loud. "I volunteered."

Willow snorted indelicately. "No way. Volunteering isn't in your DNA. Tell me what really happened."

He was a little offended she thought he was lying. "I've offered to help with things before."

"Oh, please! Wanting to run a kissing booth isn't helping. It's a celebration, not a carnival game to see how many skirts you can go up."

He grinned when she reminded him of his proposal from the previous year. He'd done it on a dare and to get under her skin. He didn't know what she did with the proposal, but would bet she incinerated it with a touch of her finger.

"I thought the kissing booth was a brilliant idea. I would have let you cut to the front of the line every time. I know you've been dying to kiss me."

Instead of smiling, her frown deepened. She shook her head and a look of disappointment washed over her face. "When are you going to grow up?"

He opened his mouth to answer, but she cut him off. It was a good thing too, since he didn't think she'd like what he had to say.

"Never mind. Don't answer that. I swear, you have Peter Pan syndrome. Back to this partner thing, I don't need your help, so I absolve you of your obligation."

"Nice try, but that isn't going to work, Wills. I gave my word to the coven I would help you out, and that's exactly what I'm going to do. I never go back on a promise."

"Stop calling me, Wills. I'm a girl, damn it."

Her temper flared and Cedric's dick responded. Hell, it responded to most things she did, but when she was feisty — it turned him on even more. She would be a spitfire in bed; he just knew it. He couldn't stop the smirk curling the corners of his mouth. Nor could he stop himself from moving into her personal space. The dig about not ever having a good moment with him replaying in his mind, eating away at him. He would give her something to remember with fondness. "Trust me. I know you're a woman," he said, his voice thick with lust.

He wrapped a hand around the nape of her neck and pulled her to him. A soft gasp escaped her lips. Her hands landed on his chest. And their pelvises made contact when she stumbled forward. The action pulled a tortured groan from him. If he thought he was hard before, he was sorely mistaken. His dick filled beyond its limits, and he swore it would burst through the zipper of his jeans at any moment. It was pure heaven and complete agonizing hell. He wanted skin-to-skin contact. Her breasts pressed into his chest. Her silky smooth legs wrapped around his waist. His hands on her delectable ass, as he rocked into her.

Without letting much thought go into his actions, he dipped his head and brushed his mouth against her slack one, once then twice. He felt her respond, bringing her lips together grazing his, and a shiver worked down his spine. As he pressed into her mouth with his tongue, he felt something zap his ankle. It wrapped around both of his feet and pulsed up his legs in small shockwaves of needle-like pain.

He shoved away from Willow and looked down at his feet, sure he would see a live wire or dragon's tail wrapped around them somehow. Neither of those was there. There *was* a larger than normal black cat curling around his legs, butting and rubbing its head against him.

"What the fuck?" Cedric stepped back to get away from the creature, but it followed him, letting out a plaintive meow. It threaded between his legs, rubbing its big body against him. More waves of pain shot up through him. It was as if the cat was trying to scare him away.

Willow chuckled. "Edward, stop. You can't have his powers." Willow bent and scooped the power-hungry kitty up into her arms, nuzzling her face into its fur. "Or, can you? He *is* a warlock after all. Is that what you were?"

Cedric stood dumbfounded as she cuddled the creature. "He's a familiar?"

Willow's dark eyes collided with his; they flashed silver for a second, then she blinked it away. He wasn't sure if it was a trick of his mind or real.

"Yes. Most witches and warlocks have one. You should know that, even though you don't."

"I didn't want one. And most of the witches end up falling in love with their familiar; the creature shifts and turns into the man or woman of their dreams."

"Yeah. So?"

"So, you haven't?"

Willow laughed. "Goddess no. Edward isn't your typical familiar."

He eyed the beast again. Yeah, he could see that. Black, soul-sucking eyes stared back at him. The cat shimmered in her arms, shifting from black to deep purple. That was not a normal familiar. "How do you know?"

She looked down at the fur ball in her arms, and tilted

her head to the side in thought. A   smile tugged at his lips. She had been doing that move since elementary school. A trait of hers he found completely endearing...once he stopped making fun of her for doing it. When she looked back at him, her brows were furrowed. "I don't know. I just know that isn't my path with him. I got him from my Aunt, who said she got him from her mother, who got him from *her* mother. You get the picture. He's been with the family for so many generations that we aren't even sure how he came to us." She shrugged like it wasn't a big deal, but Cedric made note to keep an eye on it. He wouldn't put it past the cat to try and suck every last bit of power from him while he wasn't looking. He might possibly feel it though.

"Anyway, back to the issue at hand and your reason for being here. I don't need help, so you can leave," she said.

"Sorry, babe. You're stuck with me until after the Summer Solstice." And, hopefully, beyond that if he could convince her they were destined to be together, which he fully believed. There was a reason he never let her drift away like all of the other women over the years. A reason she was never far from his thoughts.

He wanted her in his life permanently, as in forever, never going to let her go. His desperation to have her was what drove him to fix up Perry, her previous partner, and sneak his way back into her life. He was ready to grow up, but only if she was along for the ride.

Willow stared at the puzzling man in front of her. She didn't believe he wanted to help out of the goodness of his heart. There was always an ulterior motive when it came to

Cedric, at least in regards to her.

She gave him the perfect out, yet he wasn't taking it. That perplexed her some, but she figured he was trying to make a good impression on someone, she just didn't know who. Then, he had to go and kiss her, compounding her conflicting feelings about the man even more. She loved him. She hated him. It was a constant battle of wills.

What the hell was she supposed to do? She should be mad at him for that shit date, and numerous other things over the years, but she found it difficult. She had actually missed his stupid face, even though the only way she would admit it was if someone held a gun to her head…or a wand with bad intentions.

Edward shimmered again, his body vibrating with a deep purr. He only did that when he siphoned magic from someone, but he had never done it to her. It could have been a reaction from siphoning from Cedric. She'd have to make note of it in the "Magical World of Edward" book her family was compiling.

She had often wondered about his lineage, and how he came to be a part of the Davies family, so she suggested they start piecing his life together. She would jot down this reaction and get back to it later to add more details. She needed to deal with one too-handsome-for-his-own-good warlock first.

Edward lifted his head, his dark eyes flashing, a bright purple ring forming on the innermost part of his irises for a moment before turning back to their normal, eerie solid black. He meowed and wiggled in her hold.

She glanced at Cedric, who didn't look like he would leave anytime soon. She had a ton of work to do, and she couldn't stand out on the front porch forever. She might as well invite him in and then proceed to ignore him. Not that she ever had luck doing that. "I can't believe I'm saying this but—do you want to come inside?"

Cedric grinned; flashing his straight, white teeth, and her heart skipped a beat. "I thought you'd never ask."

She waved him through, and shut the door. "Let's go to the kitchen, so I can get back to work. You can do…whatever it is you think you need to do."

He nodded and walked ahead of her.

"Kitchen is straight back," she reminded him, in case he thought to veer off course and poke around her house. The less space he invaded, the better. He had only been inside her home once before. He'd dropped by the previous month with the giggly eighteen-year-old he was banging. He had wanted Willow to teach the girl a couple of sex spells. Needless to say, it hadn't gone well.

Thoughts of sex had her focus dropping to his ass. He had one of the finest asses she had ever seen. His jeans molded to his backside as if custom made strictly for him. The smooth pockets were in the perfect position, broadcasting to the population the exact spot to grab on to. She caught herself imagining sliding her hands into his pockets and wondering if he wore boxers, briefs, or went commando. She shook the thought from her head. She didn't need to get caught staring. It would only give him something else to tease her about.

CHAPTER FOUR

Jun 2nd – Tuesday

Cedric glanced at the clock in Willow's kitchen, the huge
monstrosity slowly ticking the seconds by. Had they really
only been sorting through the proposals for two hours? It felt
much longer than that, and he was bored out of his mind.

He'd taken a seat at her kitchen table with the burn of
her stare lighting him up. He doubted she knew he'd seen
her staring. Hell, he'd felt it before he glanced back and saw
her eyes lowered and riveted to his ass. It was good to know
she wasn't immune, since she hadn't mentioned the kiss on
the porch.

Now, though, his ass was numb and he wanted to kiss
her again. Ignore all of the papers and find a way to get her
naked and writhing beneath him. Maybe take things to the
bedroom where he could, once and for all, lay claim to the

one thing he'd wanted since high school.

He cast a glance in Willow's direction. She poured over another proposal and snorted in disbelief. It was probably another asinine one. He now understood her frustration about his kissing booth idea. What the hell were people thinking when they came up with the stuff they wanted to do during the annual celebrations?

A toad-changing contest: from witch/warlock to toad and back. It was a recipe for disaster if a person changed someone they were pissed at. He could imagine exes going after each other and calling it fine…all in the name of fun.

Broom races. While entertaining for youngsters, this one was geared toward adults. After hours when the mead flowed freely, drunken witches and warlocks on magic highs were no fun.

Cedric flipped the two papers into the reject pile and grabbed the next one.

A witch pageant featuring spells casting, hexing, and… bikini and evening wear. He reread it to make sure he had seen it right the first time. He glanced down the long sheet listing each event in detail to see his name written in bold at the bottom.

What the hell? How did his name end up on it?

He read a little further. The witch who proposed the pageant wanted him to be the judge *and* the prize. A witch he had dated in high school before he knew better. Her over-the-top flirting and entitled attitude left a sour taste in his mouth. She was also a witch who had teased Willow mercilessly throughout high school.

He glanced at Willow out of his periphery. She was immersed in whatever she was reading. Thank goodness. He folded the paper and shoved it in his back pocket. If he wanted her to see he was serious about her—when he got around to telling her his feelings—the last thing she needed to see was something that looked like he designed it with an ex-girlfriend. Willow would assume he and Gemma had come up with it together as a way to taunt her. His showing up and *volunteering* would be construed as a way to get around her.

He made a show of shuffling the pages around to cover up what he was doing and snatched up another proposal.

Transfiguration demonstration—okay that was a good one. He handed it off to Willow. "This one looks promising."

Without looking up, she took it from him, her fingers gliding over his in a light caress, which sent heat flaring between them. Her breath hitched, and she brought her head up.

"What the hell was that?" He asked, wondering if it had to do with the moonstone or if it was their natural chemistry. He needed to know the purpose of the stone; there was no way around it. He needed to confirm the nagging thoughts in the back of his mind.

Willow's large green eyes zeroed in on him briefly before she bit her bottom lip and dropped her gaze, looking everywhere but at him. It was her *tell* for when she was nervous. He'd figured it out in high school. She did it around him all of the time, but he didn't think anything of it. When he noticed she did it after teachers called on her, or if she had to speak in front of the class, it clicked into place. He then made it his mission to see her do it all of the time. There was something about her teeth sinking into that lush red lower lip that entranced him. "I don't know," she said, her voice almost too low to hear.

He narrowed his eyes, his gaze dropping to the moonstone dangling from her necklace. "What did you do?"

Her hand went up automatically, and her eyes skittered back to his face. "I don't know what you're talking about."

"Yes, you do. You're wearing a moonstone, Wills. Don't act like you don't know what that means, or think that I don't know. Did you enchant it? Put a spell on it? Are you trying to find true love?" A ball of tension knotted in his stomach at the thought. If she had cast a love spell on it, there was a good chance it would go horribly wrong. None, and he meant *none*, ever went how they were supposed to.

She licked her bottom lip and her face flushed. "No."

There was too much denial in that one word…paired with the reddening of her cheeks…shit, it didn't look good. "Oh god, you did," he groaned. The ball of tension turned to panic. It rose up into his chest like bile, hot, burning pain that made you want to throw up. "Take it off," he demanded. "Take it off now and undo whatever you did before it's too late."

"No." Willow pushed away from the table and scurried

over to the stove. As much as he enjoyed watching her backside when she walked away, he needed to see her face. She was horrible at lying to him. The truth always played out on her face, and he needed to see it now.

Cedric took a deep, calming breath and got up from his chair. He walked over to her and placed gentle hands on her shoulders, turning her to face him. He couldn't stress how much of a bad idea it was to place a spell on the moonstone. He never thought he would have to. "Talk to me, Wills."

Anger and embarrassment drifted over her features. The lines around the edges of her mouth pinched, and a flash of pain reflected in her eyes. "Why? What do you care if I'm trying to find someone?" She pushed his hands away and took a half step back. That was all the room she had behind her otherwise she would have kept moving.

He edged forward, closing the distance between them. "Because I do care. I don't want to see you get hurt."

"I won't," she said, tilting her head up imperiously like a queen. "The Goddess will protect me."

"I wouldn't put that much faith in them. You know playing with Mystics and humans is a game to them. They'll promise you one thing and deliver it, but it will be skewed."

"Like you," she mumbled, but he heard both words. He knew she hadn't meant to say that out loud, by the look on her face. Her eyes rounded and she clamped her lips shut.

"I'm not skewed," he frowned.

She wrinkled her cute nose, and he was tempted to run his thumb over it to smooth it out. "That's not what I meant."

He chose to ignore what she meant in favor of proving he was right. "So, you're saying you *did* do something to the moonstone?"

"We're back to that?"

"We never left the topic. This whole thing has been about that stone hanging from your neck. What did you do, Willow, so I can fix it?"

"I don't need it fixed. She promised me I would get what I want."

"She who? And what did you want?" Her answer would dictate what he needed to do. Pray. Plead. Invoke. The options were endless so he needed it narrowed down. Because whatever was needed, he would do it. He would do anything for her.

"I invoked the Goddess Aphrodite. I'm sure you can figure the rest out from there." She crossed her arms over her chest in a protective manner. Unconsciously shielding her heart. "There. You happy?"

Her answer surprised him, even though it shouldn't have. He had suspected she wanted to find love. It was a good thing Aphrodite was known for helping those who worshipped her. It was a coup for the Goddess that humans and Mystics still held her in high regard. That they offered their fealty and undying love. Many of the other Gods and

Goddesses didn't have such luck, having been forgotten over the centuries.

And yeah, he was happy. He got his answer and was pretty fucking pleased. Since his realization that he loved her, he had been wracking his brain to find a way to get close to her and tell her. Coming right out and saying it would lead to her laughing in his face in disbelief. That's when he thought to partner with her; but that would only last for so long, a week at best. He could finagle more time during the week before the big bonfire; after that, he was out of ideas. As much of a ladies man people seemed to think he was, when it came to Willow, he knew she wouldn't fall for a pretty line wrapped with a bow. She would need convincing. The stone and invocation gave him a place to start. Depending on when she performed the rite. "When did you invoke the Goddess?"

Worry creased her forehead. "Last night."

"I see." And he did. She might think his showing up was because of the rite. He knew differently, but pointing out that she wanted love, and he was the man to show up might just work in his favor.

Willow's eyes narrowed dangerously. "What do you see?"

A slow smile curled his lips. "You asked Aphrodite, the goddess of love, to help you find love, and here I am. Like I said before, the man of your dreams."

"No." She shook her head and licked her lip. Her eyes widened with alarm. "Not the man of my dreams. We've

43

already had this discussion."

He moved into her personal space again, cupping the sides of her face with his hands. He brushed his thumbs along her heated cheeks. "You're lying. You've had it bad for me since kindergarten, when you punched me in the face."

Her green eyes flashed silver and her mouth dropped open. "You deserved it, and…and I have not, she stammered." She protested, but he knew the truth. He read it in her eyes, and with each flash of silver; he knew he had her heart. He just needed to get her to admit it.

"No need to deny it, babe. I'm more than happy to fill the position." He lowered his head and brushed his lips against hers. She whimpered softly, and *wholly fuck*, it made his balls ache.

Willow didn't know what happened. One minute she was trying to get away from those all-seeing eyes of his; the next, she was melting against him, turned on like never before.

The moonstone heated against her skin, the warmth pulsing through her chest and down through her extremities. Fire built in her veins. Her blood bubbled and thickened. She could hear her heartbeat pounding in her ears. It was the single most overwhelming and addicting feeling in the world.

That's when one thought, one very important thought tumbled to the forefront.

Oh shit! He's the one!

Her brain scrambled and told her to push Cedric away, to make a scathing remark and toss him from her home. He couldn't be the one she was looking for. The one who filled the hole in her heart and sang to her soul. He was her mortal enemy. Her nemesis. The boy that never once said a kind word to her without some devious thought behind it: A favor, a sick thrill, or a cheap laugh. But her body disagreed with her mind and was ultimately the one in charge at the moment. She slid her hands up his chest, getting her first feel of the body she'd only glimpsed through the tight-fitting T-shirts he favored. The play of muscles beneath her fingers was better than she'd imagined.

She moaned against his lips, urging him on. Knew if she had to say the words, she wouldn't be able to. As it was, she cursed the sound that escaped and for falling into him so quickly. He really was the man of her dreams, even though in them, he whispered sweet endearments and was the one protecting her heart, not breaking it.

Her entire relationship with him, the anger she felt toward him was really anger with herself. For falling for a man who would never see her as more than the girl he liked to torment throughout their school years and well into adulthood.

Cedric groaned and slipped his hands down her neck and over her shoulders. They coasted down her back until he cupped her ass, pulling her close. Her body tingled all over, goosebumps danced across her flesh. The proof of his arousal pressed insistently against her belly. She didn't know he could have that reaction to her, but it thrilled her nonetheless.

She broke for air and rested her forehead against his chest. "This is crazy," she panted, running her hands down his sides, sliding them into the back pockets she had obsessed about earlier. Her left hand came up against paper, crinkling as her fingers brushed over it.

She leaned back to look him in the eyes. "What's that?" When she'd followed him into the kitchen earlier, she hadn't noticed a paper sticking out. No outline or any indication he'd had anything in his pocket. And believe her, she would have known.

He gripped her wrist and held her hand in place. "It's nothing. Something I stuffed in my pocket before I came over."

"You're lying. There wasn't anything back there. I would have noticed."

He grinned like a delighted schoolboy seeing his first pair of boobs.

It distracted him enough she was able to pluck the paper out of his pocket and break his hold on her wrist. She unfolded it quickly and edged away from him. It was one of the proposal forms. "Why do you have this?"

"Give that back," he said, trying to snatch it away.

She dodged him and rushed into the living room, scanning the page as she went. "Oh, my god." She looked up to see Cedric braced in the doorway between the kitchen and living room with a grimace on his face. Her heart dropped into her stomach. Nausea making it tumble uncomfortably. "Oh, my god, I'm so stupid." She closed her eyes so she didn't have to look at him. "It was all a ploy, wasn't it? Coming over here and playing nice. Telling me you volunteered to help and distracting me with kisses. You knew about this, didn't you?"

"It isn't what you think, Wills." He stepped toward her.

"Oh, sure it isn't. It isn't Cedric the Great lowering himself to flirt with poor pathetic Willow so she'll approve an event where he's the door prize for a bunch of horny witches. That must have been a dream come true. Did," she looked at the paper to see who submitted the idea. Of course, it would be someone who had tormented her growing up. "Did Gemma tell you that was her plan, or did the two of you come up with it together?"

"Come on, babe," he pleaded.

"No. Stop calling me babe! I'm not one of your floosies that you don't have to bother learning their name because they'll be out of your life before they know it." Her breath came in rapid bursts, and not for the reason it had before. No, she was so damn angry with herself for falling for his bullshit. For allowing a moment of weakness to seep through, and succumbing to the gentle, loving brush of his lips against hers. The paper in her hand burst into flames. She rushed to the fireplace and tossed it in. "You need to leave," she said, her voice tight. Pointing at the door, it popped open with a little help from her powers.

Cedric stopped in his tracks. "Willow, you need to let me
47

explain."

"No, I don't need to do anything, except be grateful you were by yourself this time. Wasn't my humiliation a couple of weeks ago enough to tide you over? Is your life so dull that I'm your only entertainment?" The heat of embarrassment flushed her cheeks. Her ears felt like they were on fire. And the hot press of tears threatened to spill. She held on though. She wouldn't let him see her broken heart—again.

What a fool she had been for those few blissful moments. He was using her as a means to an end…as usual.

Cedric frowned and shook his head. "I can see you aren't going to listen to me, or even believe what I say. This," he motioned between them, "isn't done by a long shot. I had nothing to do with that proposal, and I stuffed it in my pocket so you wouldn't see it. I knew you'd react this way. I want nothing to do with Gemma and *everything* to do with you. There's something between us, Willow, and I won't let you ruin it." He went to the door and stopped, throwing a frustrated, lust-filled gaze her way. "I'm in love with you damn it, and I'll prove it to you, even if it takes my last dying breath."

CHAPTER FIVE

Jun 7th – Sunday

Willow sipped her tea and stared out into her back yard. She had just finished telling Celeste, who had dropped by unexpectedly, what happened with Cedric, and waited for her reaction. Celeste knew about everything that happened between her and Cedric. She was one of the few people outside the witch community she could talk to about him without people singing his praises.

Cedric's visit still didn't make sense to her. The weird out-of-the blue arrival. His volunteering to help her out. *Fat lot of good he's been at that.* His outburst, claiming he loved her before storming from her house. What man tells a woman he loves them then storms off like a three-year-old throwing a tantrum?

She had been embarrassed and pissed off thinking he

had been trying to take advantage of her, but she wasn't any longer. She was straight up confused by his behavior now.

That had been five days ago, and she hadn't heard a word from him since. No texts. No calls. No popping in unannounced. Complete and absolute radio silence, so the speak. She was beginning to wonder if it had been a figment of her overactive imagination.

In the time he'd been gone, she had finished going through the proposals and filled in the calendar for the celebration. A tentative schedule for each day had been started, and the arrangements for the final bonfire were falling into place.

"His last dying breath?" Celeste asked, sipping her tea. She rubbed her hand absently over her lower stomach.

Willow was dying to ask if her friend were pregnant, but figured she would offer up her own gossip first. "That's what he said. It's absolutely *not* how I imagined a man telling me he loved me for the first time would be. I haven't heard from him since."

"That's so weird."

"I know. I don't even know what to do about it. I'm not mad now that I have some distance from the situation. He seemed genuinely upset about the proposal, and I know he hasn't had anything to do with Gemma in a long time. I would have heard about it from that cow's mouth if they were together."

"Gemma is that girl from high school, right? The bitchy

one that used to make fun of you because of your frizzy hair and crooked teeth?"

"Yep."

"That bitch," Celeste said under her breath. "I hate girls like that. Queen Sheba's who think they're entitled to everything just because they got breasts before the rest of the female population in school."

Willow tilted her head and looked at her friend. "You had one of those too?"

"Patience, and she was a royal pain in my ass, sticking her boobs in everyone's faces."

They laughed, and Willow felt some of her tension ease. She finished her tea and set the mug down.

"Maybe he dropped dead when he got home," Celeste offered, apparently thinking about the Cedric thing still.

Wouldn't that make things easier? *Probably not.* Willow snorted. "That would certainly explain his absence."

The both chuckled and fell into silence. Celeste sighed, and Willow figured it was as good a time as any to see what was up with her friend. "Are you ready to tell me why you stopped by unannounced? Not that I have a problem with it," she hurried to say. "I'm always up for a visit from you."

Celeste blushed. "Am I that obvious?"

"Just a little. You have a new man in your life, and
51

you're sitting with me drinking tea, which I know isn't your favorite. I figured you two would still be shacked up having lots of hot faerie sex. I'm going to guess it has something to do with you rubbing your belly."

Celeste looked down, her hand stopped moving. When she looked back up, she had a goofy grin on her face. "I'm pregnant."

"I figured as much." She leaned over and hugged her. "I'm so happy for you." And she was, along with a wee bit of jealousy.

"Thank you." Celeste beamed, and a couple sparks of faerie magic popped into the air. She chuckled softly as they danced around. "It's the hormones. I don't remember my mom having this problem. Though it could be because Owen is an elf and my dad is a human."

"It's cute."

"Yeah. Owen thought so too. At least until they turned red, and I flipped out on him for some dumb reason that I can't even remember."

"I'm sure he learned his lesson."

Celeste giggled. "Oh yeah."

Edward took that moment to hop up on the table and bat at the soft flickering lights floating in the air. He caught one on his paw and ate it. His fur shimmered, and a delighted purr rumbled from his throat. He pounced after the others, batting one into Willow's face.

She brushed it away with a flick of her hand. "Silly cat," Willow said. She turned her attention back to Celeste, who was smiling at Edward, her affection for the furball easy to see. "How did Owen take it? You two haven't been together very long."

"Oh, he's thrilled. I got the impression he was trying to knock me up. The condoms would magically disappear."

"Seriously?"

Celeste nodded, a silly smile on her face.

"Now what? Are you two getting married?" For the second time that day, Willow had to push her jealousy aside. The way things were going for her, she wouldn't be getting married. She had been wearing the blessed moonstone for almost a week, and the only man to show up was Cedric. She doubted he would be interested in a long-term relationship that resulted in white picket fences and babies.

"In time. We still have to tell my parents about the pregnancy. As it is, Mom is pushing for us to get married... sooner rather than later. Owen told his parents right after we found out this morning. But they want us to hold off for a little bit, like until *after* the baby is born. They want us to get to know each other a little better."

"Wow, that's — awkward. I'd say you two know each other pretty well. It sounds to me like you're made for each other."

"Yeah, I think we are. He wants to get married now, but I told him I want to wait until after the Summer Solstice at

53

least. I'd like my friend to be able to come." Celeste reached out and squeezed Willow's hand.

"Thanks."

"And hey, maybe by then you'll have your own hunky man to bring with you." A teasing light shone from Celeste's eyes.

Willow snorted. "Unless he dropped dead, which given the circumstance, might not be a bad thing."

"Oh? Why do you say that?"

"Life with Cedric would have been…challenging. I have a hard time believing he's serious as it is. He's tormented me for so long that I can't help but think this is another way for him to annoy me."

"Oh, come on, Willow, you like a challenge. How else do you explain teaching flighty faeries how to harness their magic? Besides, maybe Cedric flirts with you like a five-year-old on the playground. He pulls your pigtails and waits to see what happens."

"Well, the last time he pulled my pigtails, we *were* five and I punched him in the face. His tactics have changed but I don't think they've improved."

They both laughed, and any further talk was interrupted by a knock at the front door.

"I wonder who that is?" Willow mused, pushing away from the table.

54

Celeste followed behind her. "Could be Owen, but I told him I would meet him at home before we went to my parents for dinner. We're going to tell them tonight."

"Oh, to be a fly on that wall."

"Right? I expect screaming of two varieties: overjoyed and raging denial."

"Let me guess. Your mom and Avery, in that order."

"Yep."

Willow shook her head. Celeste's youngest sister would be a trial on anyone's nerves. Pampered and with a feeling of entitlement, the girl insisted Owen was her man regardless of what he said. "Your sister needs boot camp for wayward Mystics."

"I might suggest it."

"What about your dad? What do you think he'll do?"

Celeste pursed her lips. "Pass out. It should be our most exciting Sunday dinner yet."

A hard knock came from the door again.

"He's insistent," Celeste commented.

"Must be your man then. The people who come to see me knock, wait for a second, then knock again even louder." Willow opened the door, fully expecting to see Owen, but instead had all the breath knocked from her. Cedric stood on her front porch in a drool-worthy tight shirt that clung to his broad shoulders, and a pair of black slacks that hugged his thighs nicely. Shiny black dress shoes adorned his feet, completing the panty-melting look.

Willow stood unmoving. Her mouth opened and closed, and not a single thought flitted around in her head. He looked, and was, stunning.

Celeste cleared her throat and stepped up beside her. "Hi. I'm Celeste. Willow's friend."

Cedric grinned politely and held out his hand. "Cedric Stone."

"Oh, I know who you are."

A grin lit Cedric's face and Willow blushed, her cheeks heating painfully. She wanted to slap her hands on them to hide the affect he had on her but figured it would add fuel to his fire.

Celeste snapped her fingers in front of Willow's face. Willow turned her head, her brows furrowed.

"I guess he didn't drop dead," Celeste said, a bit of mischief in her voice. She hugged her and left. "Call me with details," she hollered as she walked out to her SUV parked at the curb.

Cedric soaked in the sight of a stunned Willow. She was as gorgeous as ever, but definitely not dressed for dinner out. The worn jeans and loose T-shirt were cute and looked comfortable as hell, but weren't the right attire for where they were going.

Without waiting for an invitation, he stepped into the house. He grabbed her by the hand and shut the door behind him. "Bedroom," he grunted and pulled her along with him. He stepped toward the stairs, but she yanked him back

"No," she said, tugging her hand to no avail.

"Don't bother. I'm not letting go. You and I are going out to eat, and we don't have a lot of time to get there. Reservations are at five."

"I don't remember agreeing to go out with you."

"I didn't ask." He had a feeling she would have said no if he had. That was why he went with the element of surprise.

Her dark eyes narrowed and lips tightened. "What the hell is going on, Cedric?"

He turned so they were face-to-face. "You refused to listen to me on Tuesday."

"And? It isn't the first time I've tried to tune you out. Probably won't be the last either."

"Woman, you try my patience."

"Ha! I won't even tell you what you do to mine."

Cedric closed his eyes for a moment. This wasn't going

how he'd planned. He wanted to come over and ask her out to dinner. She would say yes, she would be delighted to go. They would head to his favorite place where he could impress her a little. He could apologize for his actions on Tuesday, and say he should have just tossed it on the discard pile. In hindsight, stuffing it in his pocket made him look guilty. She would tell him she overreacted, and they could kiss and make up.

He *really* wanted to make up.

But before he had a chance to asker her, her friend made that remark about him not being dead. No idea what that was about, but it meant she talked about him. Showed he was on her mind. It eased the knot that had been in his chest since he left earlier in the week and his plan fell to the wayside.

He opened his eyes and took a calming breath. "Willow, would you do me the honor and go to dinner with me? I made reservations at new restaurant for us at five o'clock. I'd love the chance to sit down over an excellent meal and talk. Nothing more. Nothing less. I want to clear the air, as well as talk about the progress for the Summer Solstice. I made a promise to help, and I aim to keep my word."

Willow turned her head slightly, her eyes narrowed as she studied him. He could see her turn what he said over in her mind. Preying on her commitment to the coven and the upcoming event was a little underhanded, but he needed leverage to get her to say yes. He let go of her hand, figuring dragging her kicking and screaming wasn't the best way to approach with her.

58

She bit her lower lip and looked him up and down. He willed his body not to react to her perusal, but it was damn hard. *Hard. Fuck!* Hard made him think of his dick, which was in a constant state of arousal since he'd left. It stirred in his pants the longer she stared at him, and he was sure she could see the effect she had on him.

She nodded her head slowly. "Okay, but only because we need to talk about work. I'm going to assume by the way you're dressed I need to change."

He let out a relieved breath. "Yes."

"A nice outfit?"

"Yes."

"I'm not sure I have one," she warned.

Hope sprang in his chest. She was giving his invitation serious thought. "Let me help you choose. You know, so you don't feel over or under dressed."

"Okay," she said, caution lacing her voice. "But only because I don't know where we're going. Unless, of course, you'd like to tell me."

"And miss helping you out? No."

"Figures. You know High Priestess Nevaeh chastised me when I gave her my update, and she discovered we haven't been working together. I don't know how you managed to get her wrapped around your finger, but I shouldn't have been surprised."

A part of him wanted to feel bad for getting her in trouble, but the other part of him was happy to see the High Priestess actually *was* on his side, even if it was unknowingly. "Let's get you dressed."

"I'll dress myself. You're only in my bedroom to see if there is something appropriate in my closet. If not, the date is off."

Willow headed toward the back of the house, and took a right down a small hallway he hadn't noticed on his last visit. Tucked neatly under the stairs were two doors. He would guess one was storage and the other her bedroom.

When she opened the one directly in front of her and walked inside, he had to stop just short of the threshold and take a breath. An unfamiliar feeling bubbled in his chest. Nervousness. Excitement. Anticipation. It was all jumbled together.

"Are you coming, or what?" She asked from deep within the room.

He felt like a little boy about to get his innermost secret wish. He stepped inside and immediately felt seduced. The room was done with deep dark chocolate walls and crisp white trims. A large, four-poster king size bed was tucked up close to the inner wall, with a satin brown comforter. A tall highboy dresser was catty-corner to it on the far wall. Matching side tables were on either side of the bed, with elegant beaded lamps. It had feminine touches with fuzzy pillows and filigree frames scattered about, but not too much that he felt out of place. There was opulence to the room that surprised him. Not that his Willow wasn't beautiful or tasteful. He just figured the comfortable furnishings in the living and dining room would bleed over to her bedroom.

"Does it meet your approval?" She asked, leaning against the doorframe that lead, he assumed, to her closet and bathroom. Humor danced in her eyes.

"It's not what I expected."

"It never is," she said. Her mouth curved into a sexy little grin. "Closet is this way. I figure you can see if there's something suitable while I put some make-up on. Wouldn't want to embarrass you in public by looking drab." She turned and disappeared. He should assure her that would never happen but didn't think she'd take him seriously.

He followed her, stepping into a short passageway. Pants were hanging in the closet on the left; to the right was another deeper closet. He stood in the doorway of the bigger closet trying to figure out where to start. Two racks of clothes greeted him. Spending time in a woman's closet wasn't something he did on a regular basis, but he doubted most of them looked like hers.

Willow had everything sorted by type of clothing, then by color. On the left, tank tops lead to short-sleeved shirts. Then came long sleeved shirts, sweatshirts and hoodies. On the right were skirts measuring from short to long. Dresses came after them, followed by jackets. It was an OCD junky's wet dream.

Tonight she would need a nice, not-too-dressy, dress. Something cute and flirty for his pleasure. Comfortable but not too revealing for her sensibilities. But then, everything in her closet was something she had picked out, wasn't it? Something she thought she would wear at some point. He ran his hand down the neat row of hangers, coming to a stop at a cute short black sleeveless dress that flared at the bottom. There was lace at the top and a slight scoop to the neck. It would be perfect.

He pulled it out and took it to her. "This should do." He held it, letting it dangle from his finger.

She inspected it quickly and nodded. "Dressy, but not too dressy. So a decent place that doesn't require a tie, which you obviously aren't wearing. You picked a black dress, so it might be a bit more upscale. I can't think of any place in town where I would need this."

"I'm still not telling you. Get dressed, Wills. Time's a ticking."

She sighed heavily and took the dress from him. She stared at him, a look of expectation on her face.

"Do you need my help?" He asked hopefully.

"No, but I do need you to leave. I'll be out in a couple of minutes."

"Aren't you going to need me to zip you up?"

A sly grin lifted her lips. "I'm a witch, Cedric. I have magic for that."

"Fine. For the record, I don't mind helping. Sometimes you need a personal touch. Make it snappy, love." He tapped his watch, then leaned in quickly and stole a kiss. He turned away and went out to the living room. He'd give her privacy — for now.

A couple minutes later — true to Willow's word — she emerged from her bedroom looking more beautiful than ever, though she probably wouldn't believe him. Her dark locks framed her face perfectly. Smoky make-up had her dark green eyes standing out. Deep red, bow-shaped lips begged him for kisses. The dress hugged her curves beautifully, and she'd even put on a pair of sexy black heels that showcased her legs.

Holy fuck! He had never seen her wear heels before. Who would have known something as simple as seeing her toned calves would be such a turn on?

His gaze coasted up her body, his eyes landing on the moonstone resting against her dress. It glowed in the soft light in the room. Calling him closer. Tempting him to pull her against him in order to lay butterfly kisses across her luminescent skin.

"Do I look okay?" She asked and bit her lower lip.

Cedric swallowed his groan and ignored the throbbing arousal coursing through his blood. "Beautiful."

She let out a pent up breath and smiled. He didn't know what she had to worry about. She was breathtaking. "Thank you," she said. "Are you ready to go?"

He nodded and she headed for the door. As she reached for her keys, something he'd never seen on her before caught his eye.

He walked up behind her and ran his hand up her right arm. The branches of a tree spread over the soft round cap of her shoulder and crept down onto her arm. Small red flowers stood out against her pale skin. "When did you get this? And why haven't I noticed before?" He traced the swirls and dips of the branches with his finger, wondering how much more there was to the tattoo. It looked as if it started somewhere on her back.

She looked down at her arm. "I've had it for over two years. I got it on my twenty-fifth birthday."

"How come I haven't seen it before?"
She shrugged and took the keys off a hook near the door. "I'm not in the habit of showing it off. I got it for me, not everyone else. I also have a healthy T-shirt addiction that covers it."

"What does it mean?" Plucking the keys from her hand, he ushered her out the door. He locked the door, and stuffed the keys into his front pocket. He wanted to ensure she stayed with him, even if he managed to irritate her. There would be no running off this time. He threaded their fingers together and walked her to his luxury SUV.

He got her settled in her seat and shut her door. Once he was settled in his own seat, he started the vehicle and reversed out of her driveway. The place he had picked out was on the edge of town, quiet and still undiscovered. It would be perfect for their first date, and a twenty-minute drive to get there, which gave them time to chat, get comfortable with each other.

For the first time that night, he breathed a sigh of relief. He had her in his SUV, and her keys were in his pocket. She was his until he took her home. He glanced at her when he got on the main road that would take them out of town. "You never answered my question."

"About the tattoo? Haven't really had a chance."

He shrugged. That was true. He'd asked the question then got her in the vehicle. "Now is a good time. We have a little bit before we get to our destination."

She thought about it for a moment. He felt her eyes on him, as if assessing his sincerity. Whatever she saw, she relented and answered him. "It represents my path as a witch. There are deep, long roots in the center of my back that represent the start of my journey and my family. The trunk shoots up the middle of my back, then abruptly curves and branches out. The crooked branches are the twists and turns I've been through. The flowers are my hopes and dreams. The spells I've mastered, and the ones falling off are the ones that have failed. It's a continual work in progress. I get new flowers and bits of the tree added each year."

Cedric nodded and glanced in her direction. "I'd love to see the rest some time."

Willow smirked, a little half smile curving her lips. "No one but my tattoo artist has ever seen the whole thing. I haven't even shown my family."

"It seems a shame to cover it up."

She shook her head. "No. Like I said. I got it for me, not

for the world around me."

He wondered if there was a way he could convince her to show him. Certainly, if he got her into bed, he'd be able to get a look. He was dying to trace the outline with his fingers. But saying that out loud would probably hurt his cause more than help.

Another thought burst in his mind when he replayed her words in his head. *No one but my tattoo artist has ever seen the whole thing.* That meant she hasn't been to bed with a man in—ages. He hadn't expected that bit of information or how pleased it made him.

They drove until they hit the edge of town, making a right turn that would take them down a dirt road toward the forest and lead them to the secluded *Callisto's*. It was a rustic, higher-end restaurant run by a food crazy Werebear Clan that lived in the mountains, and happened to be Cedric's good friends. The place was an unknown gem on the cusp of breaking out. Patrons were slowly discovering it and calling it the best restaurant in five counties. Everyone praised Joel, the co-owner and head chef, for coming up with it. What no one besides Joel knew was that Cedric was the silent co-owner. It was Cedric's concept and his money that got it off the ground.

He parked amongst a few other cars and hopped out. He rounded the hood and was pleased to see Willow waited for him. He opened the door and took her hand, helping her out of the tall vehicle.

A small smile played on her lips, and he couldn't resist kissing her. A light brush of his lips, taking care he didn't mess up her make-up.

Her eyes flashed silver, and she ran her tongue over her bottom lips. He watched as she swiped where he had just kissed her and imagined she tasted him on her.

She tipped her head to the side and studied his face. Happiness radiated from her, and he couldn't be more thrilled to know he'd been the one to make her that way. "I'm not sure what your game is, Cedric, but I'll play along—for now," she said, her voice damn near a whisper.

Cedric caught every word though and stored them away to go over later. "Shall we head in for dinner, my lady?" He bowed slightly and held out his arm.

She laughed and took it. The glide of her hand over his forearm was more like a caress, a preview of things to come later.

CHAPTER SIX

Jun 7th – Sunday

Willow looked around the restaurant, wondering how she'd never heard of it before. From the exterior, the rustic log cabin looked like an ordinary home but once inside, it oozed elevated charm. The interior was dark and earthy. Exposed beams and a high ceiling set off the deep green walls. Heavy wood tables looked like they had been cut straight from the tree. All of the tables had over-large stuffed chairs pushed up to them. It screamed comfort and masculinity while not giving the idea a person had just walked into a man-cave.

It was no wonder Cedric wanted to make sure she was dressed for the occasion. The atmosphere called for something nice but not overly done.

A curvy brunette with the most fascinating whiskey-colored eyes greeted them after she got off the phone.

A flare of interest lit the woman's face, but quickly died. "Ric, I didn't expect to see you tonight." The woman sounded genuinely surprised. About as surprised as Willow was hearing him called Ric. "It's a pleasure to see you again."

When did he start going by that? Willow wondered. She looked at him in her periphery. He didn't seem fazed at all by the woman's use of the name.

"Evening, Natalie. I have a reservation at five."

She immediately looked down and ran a long tan finger tipped with dark red nails over the book in front of her. "Yes, Stone. Party of two," she looked up and smiled. "I assumed it was your brother bringing another of his airhead dates here. You know, there are cheaper ways to get laid." She shook her head. "Follow me and I'll take you to your table."

They followed behind Natalie to a quaint little table in the back corner of the room. Cedric kept his hand on the lower part of her back, the heat of his palm radiating through her dress. It made her feel cherished in a way.

He held out her chair, waiting for her to sit before pushing it in. Taking a seat opposite of her, he turned his attention to the hostess. "Ever since Rod's fiancée broke things off, he's been sowing his oats."

"He's more than sowing oats. He's tapping every eighteen-year-old blonde he can get his hands on," Natalie said, rolling her eyes. "Have you seen the women he's been dating?"

"Bobble-headed, brainless twits who couldn't cast a spell if their life depended on it," Willow commented without thinking.

Two sets of eyes turned her way, and she blushed. "Sorry. That's the kind you usually go for, Cedric. I figured it was a family thing."

"Funny," he said drolly.

Natalie laughed and nodded her head. "That's exactly the type Roderick has been bringing in. It makes me sad for the next generation of witches."

"I know what you mean," Willow said, deciding she liked Natalie more and more. "He won't have any better luck with faeries. They have this overwhelming feeling of entitlement. So annoying."

Cedric cleared his throat. "If you ladies are done," he said with a frown.

"Oh, cheer up, Ric. Your date seems a hell of a lot smarter than your usual fare."

Natalie held out two menus, but Cedric took both and gave them back. "Just tell Joel I'm here. He already knows what I want."

"Ohhhh...arranged this one in advance. I'm impressed. Usually you let the woman pick her meal so she can see the prices." She looked at Willow. "You must be very special for him to already know what you want."

"Special in the head to keep putting up with him," Willow replied with a smile.

"I like her. You better not let any guys in the Clan get a whiff of her. You just might find some competition. I'll tell Joel you're here, and you two can get your date started." Natalie left and their waiter showed up. He filled their water glasses, then scurried off to grab the bottle of red wine Cedric had requested.

"Sooo…Ric?"

"You know I've never liked Cedric."

That was news to her. Was she living in a bubble or something? "No. I didn't know that. I've called you Cedric my entire life."

"And, you're the only one who still does," he said, not sounding bothered by it.

She wasn't sure how she felt about that. To her, he would always be Cedric. The boy who named her Wills. The kid who used to pull her pigtails. The teenager who used to do his damndest to make her feel like a fool. The man who, with one kiss, could make her forget all of the above. "Why didn't you tell me to stop?"

"I don't know, honestly."

She didn't buy it. "Come on. You have to have some idea why?"

"If I were forced to come up with an answer—which it seems I am—it would be because I liked that you were different from everyone else in my life."

A tiny bubble of happiness burst in her chest. It was silly to let it happen. She didn't know what game he was playing, but it couldn't end well. At least not for her. "You are a dangerous, dangerous man, Cedric Stone."

A sly grin lit his face, and she knew she was in trouble.

Cedric waited until the food came out before bringing up what happened earlier in the week. Hoping the food would keep her mouth busy before she blurted out the first thing that popped into her head. Like he knew she tended to do—at least with him.

He'd told her he loved her, and she either didn't hear him, or plain didn't believe him. He'd bet on the latter.

"Let's clear the air, Willow." He took a sip of wine, then set it down.

She swallowed the bite she had taken and looked at him, question glittering in her eyes. "About?"

"What happened on Tuesday. I didn't know about that proposal. Had absolutely nothing to do with that proposal. *Want* nothing to do with that proposal. I have no interest in being a pawn—prize—whatever in someone else's game."

She pursed her lips for a second. His gaze fell to them, and all he could think about was kissing her again. "Okay. I

73

believe you."

Her response had him looking her directly in the eyes. "You do? Just like that?"

She snorted. "I do," she said. She took a couple bites of her fish while he thought that through. Tried to figure out how he felt about her easy acquiescence. He was thrown off his game, along with the speech/begging he was going to do. He felt a little deflated.

"Huh. I didn't expect you to give in so quickly."

"I can be a surprising woman, Ric."

He cringed. "Cedric." Ric sounded wrong coming from her mouth.

She chuckled and finished eating her food. When she was done, she pushed her plate away and picked up her glass of wine. She settled back in her seat and looked at him, a thoughtful expression on her face.

"What's on your mind?"

"A lot, but I'm not ready to talk about most of it yet. Let's talk about the solstice celebration. That seems safe enough *and* is the reason I agreed to dinner."

He would bet she agreed for a different reason, but wouldn't argue. "Okay. Where are you at with it?"

"Let's see. I have a rough draft of the activities and events plotted out. I still need to get with Aaron at the firehouse to confirm the number of trucks and men we'll have. Ensure we have two trucks on hand for the day of the solstice for the big bonfire. And find someone to oversee the newly minted witches who tend to get a little magic drunk every year."

Cedric didn't hear anything past her mentioning Aaron. "Aaron 'the hose' Hoserman?"

She crinkled her cute little nose up. "He doesn't like it when people call him 'the hose'. It's pretty degrading, don't you think?"

"Then he shouldn't look like he should be a male stripper or have," he cast a pointed glance at his crotch and hoped she got his meaning. Talking about how he knew Aaron had a huge dick wasn't what he considered 'date' material.

"I don't mind that he does," she smirked.

"No. I'll go see him." No way was he going to let Aaron get close to Willow. Not with that lust-filled look on her face. "What else?"

"Nothing at the moment. After the schedule is approved, we'll need to get in contact with everyone and make sure they have what they need. After that, we'll pass what we have on to Hazel and she'll take it from there."

"Does that mean we can spend time together not focusing on work?" That was his ultimate goal. The work thing was to get her used to him being around and not in the annoying way he usually was.

75

"How about we concentrate on the celebration first?"

It wasn't a no. He could deal with that. "Okay. Work first, then play."

"Something like that," a tinge of worry colored her voice.

They finished their wine, and Cedric popped back to see Joel while Willow was in the ladies room. He found his friend in the office looking over some paperwork. He pushed open the door, not bothering to knock.

"Delicious as usual, man."

Joel looked up with a smirk on his face. "Of course it was. How did it go?"

"Good. She's in the ladies room. I told your sister to keep an eye out for her."

"She's really the one you want to shackle yourself to for the rest of your life?" Joel asked, leaning back in his chair.

"Yep."

"But haven't you known her forever?"

"Yep."

"Then why are you all of a sudden figuring out she's the one for you?"

Cedric could understand why Joel was questioning him. Joel had yet to find his mate and was frustrated as hell. He masked it by acting like marriage and long-term commitment were dirty words. "Knowing the woman of my soul is a bit different than you finding your mate. I don't have a beast in me trying to make a connection."

"I know that," Joel grunted. "So, how did you know?"

"Because it's Willow. There's been this thing between us since we were five that hasn't ever gone away. She's been part of my life for so long, and when Reid asked her out, it freaked me the hell out. I realized I wanted her. Had always wanted her, and not just how I wanted her in high school."

"Yeah, you were pretty obsessed with her back then."

"No I wasn't," he said, defensiveness coating his voice.

Joel threw his head back and laughed, the deep, barrel sound filling the room. He wiped his eyes as his laughter died down. "Oh my god, that was good. She was *all* you talked about back then. We could all see it."

"Why didn't you say anything?"

"And ruin the show? Hell, no. You would track her down whenever you had a free moment just to make her uncomfortable."

"Some friend you are."

"I'm a damn good friend. Who else would want to go into business with a warlock who spends most of his time

77

chasing skirts?"

Cedric rolled his eyes. "We still on for Thursday morning?"

"Yeah. I agree we need to look at expanding our marketing plan."

Joel stood and Cedric followed suit. "Good. I'll see you then."

"Yeah, you better go find your date. The waiter came back commenting on how tasty your girl smelled and mentioned the moonstone around her neck. Seth's ears perked right up at that bit of information."

"Shit. You tell that Bear to stay away. I have *got* to get her to take that damn thing off before the solstice celebrations start. Every warlock worth his magic will be all over her."

"Good luck." Joel chuckled and took off toward the kitchen.

Cedric found his date at the hostess station talking to Natalie. The two were laughing about something when he walked up behind Willow and wrapped his arms around her waist.

Seth, the massive black bear who looked like he should be playing professional football and not chopping onions, appeared in the dining room and cast a glance in their direction.

Cedric smirked and pressed a kiss to Willow's temple.

"You ready to go home, love?"

Willow shifted to get a look at his face. "Sure," she said, though she didn't sound that way to him. She turned her attention to Natalie again, taking the card she held out. Willow passed her finger over the back of the business card and her name and phone number appeared. She held it out for Natalie. "Call me and we'll get together."

Natalie grinned, a delighted little spark making her eyes glow for a second. "I will. Good luck with him. I hear he's a *player*." She winked and Willow laughed.

"Not anymore," Cedric corrected her, getting a raised eyebrow in return. He didn't need Natalie putting that thought back into Willow's head.

He steered her out of the restaurant and into his SUV. The drive back across town was completed in silence. He figured they were both enjoying the good meal and, hopefully, each other's company.

Pulling up in front of Willow's house, he hopped out and jogged around the front. He opened her door and helped her down. With his hand pressed to her lower back, he escorted her to her porch. As much as he wanted to go inside, he figured leaving her on the doorstep would give a better impression of his intentions.

Willow turned to face him. "Thank you for tonight. I had a nice time."

"I'm glad." He dug in his front pocket and pulled out her keys. Leaning around her, he unlocked the door, pulled the keys out again and swung the door open. He took her hand and opened it, dropping the keys on her palm; he curled her fingers around them.

"Not going to invite yourself in?"

"No. I wanted dinner and to set a couple things straight. I told you that. Nothing more. Nothing less."

She nibbled on her lower lip before letting it go. She stepped into him, pressing her chest against his. He sucked in a breath, surprised by the move. Soft, light hands ghosted up his chest, tiny little shockwaves rippling through his body. Leaning in, she raised her chin, tilting her head up. Eyes closed, she kissed him. The red lips he'd stared at all through dinner were finally…finally moving against his. She started softly, sipping and sucking his bottom lip into her mouth. Her hot tongue, which still carried the taste of wine, slipped into his mouth. He moaned and gathered her against him. Eager to see how far she would go.

Fingers threaded into his hair, and she became more demanding. She held his head at the angel she wanted while invading his mouth ruthlessly. Thrusting her tongue against his, then sucking them both into her mouth. It took every ounce of willpower he had to let her stay in control. To allow her to dictate the depth and ferocity of their kiss. This was for her. A show of his restraint and continued commitment to his plan.

He felt the cool slide of his magic leave his fingers and begin to wrap around them. A warmer, more seductive power mingled with his, igniting the air around them. Pops of light burst around them like fireflies in the night. It was one of the most amazing things he ever experienced.

Willow broke their kiss and rested her head against his chest. Much like she had done once before. She panted and trembled in his arms, and he wondered if she heard the erratic beating of his heart.

He was as affected as she by the kiss.

Lifting her head, she placed a warm hand on his cheek. She leaned in and placed a whisper of a kiss on his lips before moving back. "I'll see you?"

Cedric was nodding before she finished her sentence. "Yes. Good night, sweet Willow." He forced his legs into motion and walked backwards a couple steps. "Go in the house and lock the door."

She nodded and scurried inside. He waited until he heard the door lock before going back to his SUV. Climbing in, he had to adjust his rock hard dick in order to sit. He did the best he could, but it was still uncomfortable as hell. A cold shower was in his future.

CHAPTER SEVEN

Jun 8th – Monday

Willow hung her keys back on their hook and tossed her purse down on the table next to the front door. She'd just come back from Hazel's house after an impromptu meeting to go over the schedule. Willow had the events narrowed down and needed the witch's opinion. As much as Cedric said he would help, she wanted to get it all done so she could move on with her next task. Which was informing the people who made the cut and ensuring they had everything they needed.

This year's line up was a decent mix of demonstrations, wares for sale, and carnival-type activities. Parents had to entertain their children somehow while taking part in the celebrations. Of course, those only went on during the day. As soon as the sun began to dip and the moon took over, the nighttime activities began. They were what brought in the majority of the witches and warlocks from the surrounding counties.

They would mix and mingle. Magic of all varieties would fill the air. The later the evening, the darker and more seductive it became. Clothes tended to fall away, and people let the atmosphere and draw of the moon wash their inhibitions away.

One nighttime event Willow looked forward to watching was Magical Bindings. There was something alluring and slightly illicit about being able to bind your partner with only a few whispered words. Maybe she could use them on one wily warlock who threw her perfectly ordered world out of place.

He was not how he used to be and it frightened her. Maybe...just maybe, he had grown up more than she thought. Time would tell she supposed.

Willow went into the kitchen and was greeted by Edward. He lounged on her dining table in a shaft of sunlight. His deep purr rumbled softly as he looked at her through narrowed eyes.

"I see you've been keeping yourself busy."
Edward stood and stretched. Arching his back high into the air. He flicked his tail once before hopping down, landing gracefully on four feet.

"Am I to guess you'd like a treat?" She asked as he wound his way around her feet. "I'll take that as a yes. I did leave you here by yourself, and it's been a couple of hours."

Reaching for the glass container that held his kitty treats, she opened it and grabbed a couple out. Kneeling down, she held one out. "Did anything exciting happen while I was gone? Phone calls or people dropping by?"

He let out a long meow before snatching the treat from her fingers. He looked pointedly at her hand, knowing she had more. She fed them to him quickly. Dusting her hands off and standing. He bumped against her leg in thanks then walked off.

She followed him, deciding she could get her phone calls out of the way. As she was digging her list out of her purse, there was a knock at her door.

"This place is turning into a regular train station these days," she mumbled and answered the door.

Cedric was leaning against the doorframe looking sexy as ever. He had traded his crisp white button down shirt and black slacks from the night before for one of his super tight T-shirts and faded jeans. She had to admit both looks were great on him. His hair was tumbled loosely around his shoulders. What would he think if he knew she had fantasies about his long locks? Sliding her fingers through it before she wound it tightly in her fists. Using the hold to direct him precisely where she wanted him. Sucking her breasts. Working his way down her body. Steering him between her legs, so he could bring her to orgasm with that sinful mouth of his.

She shook her head and cleared her lustful thoughts. Pasting on a bright smile she said, "And what can I help you with this fine," she glanced at her watch quickly, "midmorning?"

Cedric straightened and moved into her personal space. He dropped a quick but fiery kiss on her lips before shuffling her backwards.

The door slammed closed, and then his hands were gathering her closer. Pulling their bodies flush.

Edward, who had been lurking in the living room, wrapped his frame around Cedric's legs, making him jolt. She felt the zap jump from Cedric onto her. He pushed her back but didn't let go.

"What is with your cat?" He sidestepped Edward and turned her, switching their places.

Willow frowned and untangled her hands, which had somehow fisted his shirt. She looked down at the *familiar* circling her legs. "I don't know. He's never done that to anyone before. Most people don't even notice when he's trying to steal a little magic."

"Is that what he's doing? You need to put him on a leash or something."

Edward's meow came out like a snort. He flounced off and hopped up on the couch, choosing to ignore them. He cleaned his fur and worked his claws into the back of the couch.

"Anyway, I came to see if you wanted to head to the firehouse with me to talk to Aaron. After thinking about it last night, I figured it would be best if you were with me.

86

When we're done, I thought we could go out for lunch."

She pursed her lips and eyed him suspiciously. That hadn't been his attitude the night before. In fact, she got the impression he didn't want her near the firehouse. What could have happened to change his mind?

She wouldn't find out if she didn't go. "Is this a business lunch?"

"No. I'm asking you out again."

"I don't recall you asking me before you made plans last time." Not that she minded. The food had been delicious and the company wasn't too bad.

"No plans this time. I wanted to see you again. Thought I could ask you out to lunch, and we could wrap up the firehouse thing."

She thought about it for a moment. She was hungry. And she would have gone behind him to double check he'd done the work. "Okay. That'll mean one less thing for me to do, and I am hungry. I saw Hazel this morning and the schedule is set. I wasn't tired after you dropped me off, so I finished going through the proposals just so we could be done."

A slow grin curled those magnificent lips of his. She caught herself before she leaned in to kiss him. He had turned their relationship upside down; and she, all to easily, let him.

"Couldn't keep your mind off me, could you?"

There was the Cedric she knew. She rocked back on her heels and rolled her eyes. She turned and grabbed her keys and purse. "Let's go."

"I'm going to take your non-answer to mean you couldn't. I know I couldn't get you off my mind."

He walked out and she locked the door. Most magic-kind would look at her funny if they saw her doing it. It really only took a flick of the wrist to lock and unlock a door or window or anything really. It was a basic spell all witches and warlocks learned when they were young. And because of that, she had her door enchanted against magic.

"Let's get to the station before Aaron gets called away." She would keep *not* answering because it was true. She couldn't keep her mind from drifting to the kiss they shared on her porch, or what she wanted him to do to her…a rough push against the door, her legs wrapped around his waist. She knew he had the strength in him to keep her pinned there. To ravish her like she was the only woman for him.

The last part wasn't true. She glanced his way as they walked to his SUV. He must have felt her gaze, because he looked at her and smiled. Her heart did that silly erratic thump when the corner of his mouth lifted. Something indefinable twinkled in his eyes. It almost reminded her of pure, simple pleasure. He held her door open and helped her in. Before he shut it, he kissed her again. A gentle brush of his lips against hers. He was getting way too familiar with her.

Her door slammed, and he walked around the front. The man was undoing her quickly, and she didn't know what to do to make it stop, or if she wanted to stop it at all.

Cedric stood behind Willow as she talked to Aaron Hoserman. The man was entirely too friendly and flirty with her, and it was grating on his nerves.

The second they had shown up and found him, Aaron had ignored Cedric in favor of Willow. He took her by the arm and gave her a tour of the firehouse. The kitchen, day room where they all hung out, the hanger with all of the trucks, and lastly, the sleeping quarters.

They stood in the quiet corridor with five individual rooms on both sides. Each room had a curtained doorway to make it easier to rush out on a call. It also gave them a little privacy for anything they may need, like seducing someone else's woman.

He snapped back to the present at the sound of Willow's voice.

"You can't expect me to believe you fit on that bed, Aaron. There's no way in hell. You're too big."

Cedric whipped his head in the direction they were talking. Aaron stepped into one of the rooms, pulling Willow with him. They stood next to what he would guess was a full size bed. It had a dark comforter and a couple of matching pillows.

"Sure I do, Willow. There's even enough room for you to fit on there with me. Come lay down and I'll show you." Aaron winked, and Cedric let loose a bolt of lightning.

It arced across the floor, traveling up the metal desk and popped the light bulb in the lamp.

"Sorry about that," he shrugged and gave his best apologetic look. But he wasn't. Not one damn bit. Aaron's dark eyebrow rose, and Cedric figured he didn't believe him. "How about we talk about the arrangements for the Summer Solstice? We would like to wrap your end of it up."

He threaded his fingers with Willow's and tugged her out of the room, away from the randy firefighter.

Aaron chuckled and moved ahead of them. "Let's head to the office, and we'll go over everything."

Willow pulled on her hand, but he refused to let go. "What is wrong with you?" She hissed. Her panicked gaze bouncing between Aaron and him.

"Nothing," he replied through clenched teeth. Unless, you consider murdering someone for flirting with the woman you love wrong.

"Bullshit. What was that back there, and what's with this?" She swung their hands out in front of them. He didn't see anything wrong with them holding hands. He liked it.

"He was flirting with you. Trying to get you in bed."

Willow's brows drew down into a deep furrow. "No, he wasn't. He was just joking around."

"Bullshit," he retorted. "He's hard as hell for you."

Willow's eyes rounded quickly. "Oh, my god, you're insane. And what are you doing looking at his junk? Are *you* hot for him?"

Cedric barked out a laugh. "Love, men don't do it for me, and if you missed that damn snake in his pants, then you must be blind."

Before she had a chance to reply, Cedric's phone buzzed in his pocket. He pulled it out and checked it. "Shit, I need to take this. I'll be back in a minute." He walked off, but not too far away. Leaning up against the wall not close to the office, but with enough distance he couldn't be heard, he saw Aaron lean into Willow as she entered the room. A poisonous thread of jealousy snaked through his veins, leaving a foul taste in his mouth.

Willow cast a glance at Cedric, who was getting out of helping her once again, then turned her attention to Aaron. He held the door open for her, a big grin on his handsome face, waiting patiently. He took up so much space; she accidentally brushed her shoulder against his massive chest. "Sorry," she mumbled.

Aaron stopped her with a hand to her arm. He leaned in close. "For the record, I wasn't joking. I *was* trying to get you in bed with me." His husky whisper drifted over her ear, sending a shudder down her spine. It was mildly arousing, but nowhere close to the explosive feeling she got with the man out on the hall.

She turned her head and came face-to-face with him. "What?"

"Damn, sweetheart. I must be off my game if you couldn't tell. Your wannabe boyfriend is right."

"He's not my boyfriend," she blurted out.

His grin grew bigger. "Good. I was flirting with you, and I'm hard as hell." He raked a hot gaze that should have had her knees trembling. "You're fucking hot."

He dropped a quick kiss on her lips, then went around to the other side of the desk, planting his ass in the large, overstuffed leather chair.

She blinked repeatedly to clear the fog and confusion that had set in. Since when had Aaron ever thought she was hot? All of the other times she saw him, he was cordial enough; but he never looked at her like he was picturing her naked. Her hand drifted to the moonstone and the possible cause of this new development. It was warm, but no warmer than it should be resting against her skin. It definitely didn't react like it did when Cedric kissed her.

CHAPTER EIGHT

Jun 8th – Monday

The fresh air did wonders for Cedric's sour mood. Or, it could be that they were no longer in the firehouse and a certain firefighter couldn't hit on Willow anymore.

His jealousy knew no bounds, as the other man had a lot of nerve to flirt *and* kiss her in front of him. Apparently, his presence wasn't enough to deter other men. Not with that damn moonstone around her neck. This was exactly the thing he wanted to avoid next week, and why he needed to get it from around her neck.

"Is the café okay with you? We can sit outside," Willow said as they walked down the Main Street sidewalk.

"Sounds good." He wouldn't mind people seeing them together. Maybe they would get it in their fool heads Willow was taken.

The hostess, a girl he had gone out with once before, smiled brightly at him and told them to pick a table. She followed them out with two menus, placing them on the table before heading off to grab them water.

Like the gentleman he was, Cedric held the chair for Willow and helped scoot her in. He took the seat to her right, instead of the one across from her. Being able to touch her anytime he wanted was a necessity. Also, anyone walking by would see them together, and if he knew the citizens of the town, news of their relationship would spread like wildfire.

A smile tipped his lips at the thought. There would be no mistaking they were together by the time the solstice celebrations started. He never knew he would be so desperate for people to know he was with someone. Or, more specifically, that Willow was with him.

Willow dipped her head and studied the menu, though he doubted she really needed to. The café had been a popular spot when they were growing up. Most of them gathered there after school to hang out and be a general nuisance.

The hostess came back out and set their waters down. She stood next to him and fidgeted. He saw her twisting a ring on her finger out of the corner of his eye. He had no idea what she was still doing standing there. He looked up at her and smiled.

Relief flooded her face for some unknown reason. "It's good to see you again, Ric."

94

Cedric tried his best not to cringe, and he could have sworn he heard Willow snort when the hostess called him Ric. He kept his focus on the woman, silently wishing she would hurry up and say whatever it was she seemed determined to say.

She batted her long eyelashes at him, and he had a sinking feeling in the pit of his stomach. "I had a *really* great time on our date," she paused and licked her lips. "And I wondered if you wanted to go out again. My shift ends in a couple hours, and I'm free tonight if that works for you."

An odd sound came from Willow. It sounded somewhere between a snort and a chuckle. He cast a glance in her direction and saw her shoulders shake behind the menu she'd pulled up to cover her face. Reaching over, he plucked the menu from her hands.

Indignation played across her face. Her mouth popped open. "Hey, I wasn't done looking."

"You have the same thing every time you come here."

"How would you know?"

"Because I know everything about you, love," he smirked.

She harrumphed and crossed her arms over her chest, pouting.

He turned back to the hostess, pasting a placating smile on his face. "I'm sorry," his gaze dropped to her nametag then back to her face. "Tiffany. I'm here with my girlfriend and we're pretty serious. I won't be going out with anyone else."

The girl blinked rapidly, her mouth dropping open. "It's never stopped you before. And you weren't with her two weeks ago, how serious could it be after such a short time?" She eyed Willow dubiously, and it pissed him off.

Tiffany made him sound bad, and his tendency to date one woman after another was *not* something he needed Willow to be reminded of. "We're *very* serious," he said, putting some force behind the word. He thrust the menus at her. "Please, send our waiter over, we're ready to order."

The girl gasped, obviously hurt that he wasn't tossing Willow aside for her, then spun away.

"You didn't need to be mean about it, *Ric.*" Willow snickered, and he pinned her with a glare. He didn't like her calling him that.

"I wasn't. And what is with people? That's twice today someone assumed we weren't together."

"Twice?"

"Yeah, Tiffany and Aaron. Don't think I didn't see him kiss you. As a matter of fact." He grabbed the arm of her chair and yanked her closer. As soon as she was within range, he wrapped his fingers around the back of her neck and kissed her. Her lips softened against his instantly, parting slightly on a sigh. He took advantage and sucked her bottom lip into his mouth, nipping it lightly, then soothing it with his tongue. He pulled away and she moaned. Her eyes fluttered open and lust radiated from within.

Someone coughed next to him, bringing his attention back to where they were. Cedric turned his head and found the waiter waiting, notepad in hand. His eyes were as big as saucers.

"She'll have the Chicken Pecan Salad with the raspberry vinaigrette, and I'll have the Chicken Carbonara."

The man hurried away and Willow laughed. "I think he's scarred for life."

"Or jealous as hell."

"Maybe he wanted to be the one you were kissing. I bet he's in there relaying what he just saw to Tiffany."

"She'll get over it." He shrugged and took a sip of water. He looked out on the street and watched as people walked by. They stared at them. Some not caring. Some, people he knew, clearly surprised.

He felt Willow regarding him steadily.

"I'm not your girlfriend, just so you know," she said, running a finger back and forth over the tablecloth. The saltshaker started to dance, and he felt her anxiety like a living, breathing thing.

"Maybe I want you to be." He did, and so much more.

"No one would ever believe that."

That caught his attention. "Why not?"

The shaker he was keeping an eye on started hopping up and down in tune with her now tapping finger. "Everyone would be waiting for you to pull the rug out from underneath me and have a good laugh."

"Why would they ever think that?" He rested his hand on top of hers, the shaker stopped moving. He turned her hand over and laced their fingers together. A part of him was soothed by the intimacy, no matter how innocent it was.

She tilted her head and her forehead wrinkled. "Because that's what you do to me. Have you not been paying attention to our relationship over the years?"

"I have."

"Then what kind do *you* think we have?"

"Friendship." At least that's how *he* saw it. They joked around with each other and poked fun. There were never any hard feelings. Not on his part anyway. He had never taken the time to think or ask how she felt.

"I'm not sure you know what that word means." Her brows furrowed in confusion.

"Yes, I do. I have a lot of friends. We hang out. Do shit. Talk shit. Have each other's back when needed."

"We don't do any of that."

Shit, now he was confused. "What do you do with your

friends?"

She did a one-shoulder shrug and looked away. Her gaze landed somewhere on the passing traffic. "Go out to eat. Hang out at each other's house. Go shopping and talk. We get manis and pedis. Girl stuff, I guess."

"So, the same thing."

"Basically, but we," she motioned between them. "Don't do that. You joke around with your friends, and I end up being the butt of a joke or a horrible, cringe-worthy date. Your friends did have your back that day. They sat behind you and laughed at my expense."

That was news to him but, now that he was forced to think about it, he did recall laughter behind him at the time. He figured it was about something else. None of them said anything to him at the time. He also wouldn't have listened since he was trying to talk to Willow.

"I'm sorry they laughed. I didn't realize it was about you. Do you want me to kick their asses?"

"I don't think that's how friendship works."

"Sure it is. We're guys. We're allowed to beat each other up, and when we're done, we'll sit down and drink a beer."

"Men are strange. My whole point, though, was that I'm not your girlfriend, and you could have set up a date with the hostess if you'd wanted."

"I didn't want to."

99

"But you could have."

"And yet, I still don't want to. I'm on a date with the woman I *want* to be with."

"For now, until you get whatever has you all screwed up inside thinking you want to be with me out of your system."

"Won't happen." He picked up her hand and kissed her palm.

"We'll see," she said, doubt creeping into her voice. Her hand drifted up to the moonstone. He didn't think she knew she was doing it.

Their server reappeared and set their food down in front of them. With a nod and a thank you, Cedric dismissed him.

Willow dug into her salad, mixing it up. A companionable silence fell over them.

"For the record, Aaron has nothing on you when it comes to kissing."

Cedric whipped his head in her direction. She had a slight, close-lipped smile on her face and teasing light to her eyes. He sat up a little straighter, his chest puffed out a bit, and his ego was duly stroked.

After lunch, Cedric dropped Willow off at home. It went against everything in him to leave her standing on her front porch. He wanted to invite himself in and find a way to coax her to her bedroom. But part of a semi-slow seduction was waiting for the right time, and that certainly wasn't at the moment. He kissed her goodbye and left once again.

He also had other places to be, and a business partner to talk to. Joel had received a call from the local newspaper wanting to do a story on *Callisto's*. They needed to decide if it was time to introduce Cedric, taking him out of the silent partner sphere.

CHAPTER NINE

Jun 9th – Tuesday

Willow scrambled for her purse and the ringing cell phone inside. She wrapped her fingers around it right when it stopped.

"That's what I get for leaving it in there," she mumbled, flipping the phone over so she could see who had called. It was the number for the firehouse.

She tapped on the missed number and let it ring. Wondering if something had gone wrong and they needed to arrange for a backup.

"Firehouse 15, this is Aaron."

"Oh hey, Aaron, this is Willow. It looks like I missed a call from you guys."

103

He chuckled lightly. "Not all of us. Just me."

"Oh, okay. What's up? Is there a problem with the arrangements?"

"No. Those are still good. I was actually calling to see if you'd like to go out with me sometime. I was thinking I could take you to lunch or maybe a cup of coffee."

"Oh!" She hadn't expected him to ask her out.

"Is that a good 'oh' or bad 'oh'?"

She didn't know. He was a good-looking man, but she couldn't say she had ever thought of dating him. "It's a surprised oh," she finally said.

"What do you say, sweetheart, want to go out on a date with me?"

Willow clutched the moonstone automatically. It warmed against her fingers a little, but she questioned whether it was from a new heat source or because of Aaron. Maybe it didn't react unless she was with the man of her dreams in person.

"Sure," she said, even though something inside her hesitated. There had to be a reason Aaron was on her radar now, and if it were from the Goddess, she wouldn't turn the opportunity away. "Lunch sounds good. When were you thinking?"

"How about today? I get off shift in a couple hours and can meet you at the café."

104

A moment of guilt swamped her at the mention of the café. She had just gone there with Cedric on a date. She couldn't go there with another man. At least not so soon.

"How about *Pain et du Chocolat*? It's been a while since I've been there, and I heard they have some new menu items."

"The bread and chocolate place? Sounds good. One of my buddies said its good, and I've wanted to check it out. Want to meet there around one?"

"Okay. I'll see you then." Willow hung up and slid the phone in her pocket.

She wandered back into the kitchen and finished making her tea. She glanced at the clock. Three hours before she met up with Aaron. What in the world did she do in the meantime?

She had yet to hear from or see Cedric. The last she had heard from him was on Sunday night when he sent her a text. Was it considered stepping out on him when she didn't know what they were doing in the first place?

He said he wanted her as his girlfriend, but they hadn't talked about it. There was nothing official. She also didn't know if he was serious or stringing her along. There were just too many unknowns with him.

The moonstone made her doubt what was happening between them. He *had* shown up the morning after the rite. His new fascination could just be the pull from the Goddess of love and desire.

Willow took her tea and went into the living room. Edward followed her in and curled around her feet before jumping up onto the back of the couch.

"Well, Edward, what do you think? Is the moonstone playing a trick on my mind? Is the attention only because of it?"

Edward, the cheeky cat, batted the back of her head.

"Hey, that was rude."

He tipped his head up and looked away.

"What? You think I should be a lonely old spinster and find you a lady friend instead?"

Edward meowed and hopped off the back of the couch. He walked across her legs and curled in her lap.

"I think you like that idea a bit too much. How about we compromise? You help me figure out what is real and what is solely because of the moonstone, and I'll find you a lady cat."

Edward purred and kneaded her legs with his claws. The sharp little talons digging in none too gently.

"I'll take that as a yes."

The next couple of hours flew by and before she knew it, it was time to head to *Pain et du Chocolat*. She fluffed her hair and changed out of her fur-laden clothes. Choosing to go casual with a pair of dark jeans and a pink top. Her tattoo was covered and her makeup was done. It was as good as it was going to get for a last minute date.

She got in her car and headed to Main Street. As she parked, her phone buzzed in her purse. She quickly dug it out and saw a text from Cedric.

Wanna meet for lunch?

Her heart skipped a beat, and she ended up chewing on her lip. She was flooded with guilt for agreeing to go to lunch with Aaron, but if she wanted to find love, then she needed to take chances. She had to be honest with Cedric. It wasn't like they were actually dating. He'd taken her out for two meals, and once was after conducting coven business. In the big book of dating rules, she didn't think that counted.

Already have plans. Meeting Aaron for lunch. She shot off the text and dropped her phone back in her purse, afraid of his response. Getting out of the car, she locked it and headed across the street to the small restaurant. Aaron stood out front waiting for her.

The big man looked good. Short, brown hair cropped close to his head. Deep-blue eyes twinkling in the bright sunlight. Tight, faded jeans and a firehouse T-shirt accented his thick muscles. His biceps bulged, and she spied a tribal tattoo peeking out from one sleeve. He grinned, the left side of his mouth tipping up higher than the right.

She grabbed the moonstone and waited for a reaction. He should have been sending her libido through the roof. Goddess knew most of the women she knew lusted after the hot firefighter and his equally hot colleagues. When nothing
107

happened, she let go and pasted a smile on her face. She had a sinking feeling lunch was going to be a disaster, at least in the love department.

"Hey, Willow," he greeted her, leaning in to kiss her cheek. There was no spark when his firm lips touched her skin. He slid a hand down her back, coming to a stop right before he got to her ass. "Ready to grab some grub?"

"Sure," she replied as brightly as possible.

They were seated quickly and ordered after a couple minutes. An awkward silence fell over them as they waited for their food.

Willow pinched her lips together and grasped the moonstone.

"So…" Aaron started, but didn't say anything else. He looked at her like she should take the lead from there.

The silence was killing her. "How do you like being a fireman?" She asked, feeling ridiculous as soon as the words left her mouth. She already knew he loved it. Any fool with eyes could see that.

He chuckled lightly. "This is awkward, isn't it?

"A little and I don't know why. We don't know each other well, so you would think we'd have loads to talk about. Things to learn about each other."

"Yeah. I don't get it either. I had no problem talking to you at the firehouse."

"Maybe we aren't meant to be anything other than friends."

"Could be. I'm not too sure how that would go though. I don't know how to be friends with a woman. I pretty much end up sleeping with them and that's about it. There's no forming a friendship after you've fucked each other's brains out. All you end up doing is imagining them naked when they want to talk. From my experience, women don't like that."

Willow laughed. "I have a friend like that. Though, I've never slept with him."

Aaron sent a sly look her way. "Ric?"

"Yes."

"What's up with you two? He looked fucking pissed at the firehouse on Sunday. He definitely wasn't keen on me trying to get you in bed, or when I kissed you."

Willow shook her head. "I really don't know. He's been acting strange the last week or so. He even says he's in love with me, but I think he's going through some mid-life crisis."

Aaron's dark eyebrows shot up to his hairline in surprise. "He's in love with you? Jesus! What are you doing having lunch with me then?"

"I'm out to lunch with you because you asked, and I wanted to. But, I think we both now know nothing is going to happen between us in a romantic sense."

"Romantic? Probably not. But I wouldn't be opposed to heating up the sheets with you."

"Oh!" She hadn't expected his honesty about that. She waited for the arousal to hit her at the thought of sleeping with him, but it never did.

"But," he paused, his expression turning serious. "I don't intentionally poach on another guy's territory. I didn't think he was serious about you when you two came to the firehouse, so I thought you were fair game. I've always seen you two as oil and water and; well, he's a bit of a hound."

"That might be an understatement," she mumbled mostly to herself.

Aaron smiled knowingly. "Do I hear a bit of jealousy in your voice?"

"No," she replied, affronted by the accusation. She wasn't jealous that every other woman she knew had the attention and then some of Cedric at one point or another.

A huge grin lit Aaron's face. "Sorry, sweetheart, but I think I do. As a matter of fact, I think *you're* in love with him. Otherwise, you wouldn't have that look on your face."

"What look?"

"Like someone pissed in your cereal."

Willow rolled her eyes at the crude comment. "Goddess no. How can I be in love with someone who is constantly making my life hell?"

"Because you like it," he said, a smug smile lifting the corner of his lips. "I don't see him acting that way with other women. You must be pretty damn special to him."

Their server brought their food, ending the conversation. She was definitely *not* supposed to fall in love with Aaron Hoserman.

They ate their meals and chatted about the solstice celebration. When they were done, Aaron paid and escorted her to her car. He kissed her cheek and waited next to her car as she got in. He motioned for her to put the window down.

"I had a good time," he said, leaning down, his hand on the roof of her car.

"I did too, even if you think I'm in love with Cedric."

He chuckled. "I know you are now, if that comment is still bothering you. I hope it works out, but if he breaks your heart and you need a shoulder to cry on, I'm happy to supply mine."

"You're just hoping I'm a wreck and decide to fall into bed with you."

"Just putting it out there," he waggled his eyebrows.

"You're incorrigible. I'll see you around, Aaron. Thanks for lunch."

He tapped on the roof of the car and stood back. "Thanks for showing me I might actually be able to be friends with a woman…as long as she's taken."

Willow reversed out of her spot and drove the ten minutes home. As she approached her house, she noticed a very familiar, expensive SUV parked in front, but there was no sign of the driver.

"This should be fun." Parking, she got out of her car and made her way to the front door.

Cedric was leaning against the railing just like he had the Sunday he showed back up in her life.

She nodded at him and let herself in. He followed behind, not bothering to wait for an invitation. Keys and purse put away, she figured it would be a good time for some tea. Something to keep her hands busy as she waited for Cedric's reason for being there.

He sat in one of the chairs and waited. His eyebrow raised and a wounded look on his face. The guilt of going out with Aaron grew. In the back of her mind, she knew she was wrong, but she'd used the lame excuse that she and Cedric weren't really dating to justify it.

She made them each a cup of tea and set his down in front of him before she took her seat.

He sipped it quietly, studying her as her nerves ratcheted up another notch. His steady gaze was beginning to unnerve her.

She couldn't take it anymore. "I'm sorry," she said, not even knowing that was what was going to come out of her mouth.

"You're sorry for what?"

"The lunch date. It was a mistake."

He nodded as if agreeing, but didn't say anything.

"I knew I shouldn't have gone, even though you and I aren't really a thing. I mean, we've gone out twice, and once was after coven business. I don't think that actually counts as a date. That's two people eating because they were hungry after getting some work done."

"Are you trying to convince me or yourself? I was surprised and pretty pissed you went out with Aaron. I know I don't have a claim on you, but I thought you understood I want something more."

"More?"

"Yes. More than our current relationship that you say isn't really friendship. I meant what I said the other day, Willow. I'm in love with you. It's taken me a long time to realize that was what I felt, but it doesn't make it any less true."

"Oh." It was all she could think to say.

"Don't worry. I can wait to hear you say it back. I know you need time, but don't take too long." He sipped his tea, then let out a loud breath. She got the impression he was warring with something inside. "Can you do me a favor?"

"Of course."

"You don't even know what it is. How can you say yes without details?"

"When have I ever turned you down?"

His mouth curved into a pleased smile. "Don't go out on any more dates with other men. Aaron is pretty fucking lucky I'm not over there maiming him."

She snorted and nodded. She was fairly certain she wouldn't be seeing anyone else. The guilt she felt for having lunch with Aaron was enough to put her off.

CHAPTER TEN

Jun 12th – Friday

Willow saw Cedric every day over the next couple
of days. He would show up in the morning, sometimes
bringing a hot tea for her, sometimes just bringing himself
and a scorching kiss that left her breathless and aching
for more. They would talk and get to know each other,
occasionally reminiscing about their past.

He figured out if he brought kitty treats for Edward, he
would escape the power-hungry feline's zapping. Willow
also thought he was letting the *familiar* siphon off a little
power to keep him happy.

He was taking his time with her. She knew it. He knew
it. They didn't talk about it. She had the feeling he was
letting her get used to having him around. Each morning he
stayed a little longer, then he left to do Goddess knew what.

They didn't talk about what he did for a living. Honestly, she figured wooing women took up the majority of his time.

She smoothed her hand down the long flowing skirt she'd put on when getting ready. During Cedric's morning visit that day, he told her her had special plans for them and to dress nice. He had been tight-lipped about what they were going to do, and told her she had to trust him.

She found it easier and easier to do just that. She was beginning to believe what he said about wanting more with her. He told her repeatedly all he wanted was time with her. Nothing more. Nothing less. She thought about embroidering the saying on a pillow for him.

She heard a car pull up in front of the house. Peeking out the front door, she saw his SUV. He stepped out and strode through her lawn looking hotter than ever.

He had on a charcoal grey suit with a matching vest and crisp white shirt beneath. His tie had small black and white patterned squares. And a white pocket square was neatly folded and sticking out of the breast pocket. His shoes were black matte and perfect for the overall look.

A flicker of heat burst through her chest. He looked devastatingly good, and a hell of a lot more dressed up than last time.

Catching her bottom lip between her teeth, she wondered if she was dressed nice enough. She'd picked a white silk sleeveless top with tiny pearl buttons. Her skirt was a modern design of red, white, and black freeform shapes. She'd wedged her feet into a pair of heels that had seen action only once before—in the store. They were black and had a deep red heel that matched the skirt perfectly.

Grabbing her house key and the tiny black wristlet she'd switched to for the evening, she locked the door and waited for him on the porch. A slow grin curled Cedric's lips as he mounted the few steps it took to get to her.

"You look gorgeous," he said, his sincerity easy to hear. Wrapping an arm around her waist, he hauled her against his body. She ran her hands over his chest, unable to resist touching the soft fabric of the suit.

She tilted her head up in expectation of his kiss. He didn't leave her wanting. Lowering his mouth to hers, he brushed his lips softly against hers before lifting his head.

"Thank you." She blushed, the heat filling her cheeks. "Good enough for tonight? You were pretty cryptic this morning."

"No one will be able to keep their eyes off you." He ran a knuckle down her cheek. Every hair on her body stood at attention. The caress set her on fire.

"Let's go, love, before I drag you back into that house and ravish you."

Willow didn't think that sounded half bad, but she didn't give voice her opinion. She was enjoying his slow seduction, and part of her was afraid he would stop if he got into her bed. And maybe, in the back of her mind, she thought that might be his ultimate goal—dump her once he'd conquered her. She was enjoying him too much to put an end to whatever the hell it was they were doing. If she got a little frustrated at the speed of things occasionally, then that was *her* problem.

He threaded their fingers together and walked her to the SUV. Once he got her settled and buckled, he brushed a soft kiss against her lips. She let out a dreamy sigh as he walked around the front of the vehicle.

Twenty minutes later, they were pulling up at *Callisto's* again; except this time, the parking lot was packed. People milled about out front, chatting and seeming to wait. She spied one of those little square coaster-looking things that lit up, in a man's hand. They were waiting for a table.

"It looks busy. Maybe we should go somewhere else."

Cedric grinned down at her and tugged her along. "Nope. This is right where we need to be."

"Okay," she said, then looked around. "I don't mind waiting if you don't."

"We won't have to wait." He opened the door for her and pressed his hand to her lower back, propelling her in front of him.

Natalie was at the hostess station, along with another younger woman. Natalie looked up and saw them come in. "Willow," she gushed and came forward, enveloping her in a hug.

"This place seems to have exploded," Willow said, looking around at all of the full tables. Servers rushed around with pitchers of water and food. People talked and laughed. It was probably a restaurant owner's wet dream.

"Yeah, can you believe it? It's insane." Her focus drifted to Cedric. "And you! Why didn't you tell me sooner?"

Cedric shook his head slightly, then looked at Willow.

"Tell you what sooner?" Willow asked, looking back and forth between Cedric and Natalie.

"You'll know soon enough." He turned back to Natalie. "Is he in his office?"

"Yep. You know where it's at, and your table is ready whenever you are."

He nodded and guided her through the throng of people toward the back. He went through the *employee only* door and pointed to an office on the right. "We're heading in there."

"What deep dark secret am I about to learn?" She asked as he opened the door and waited for her to walk in.

"That he's part owner of this fine establishment." A man with a deep voice and barrel chest stood behind a desk. A lock of dark hair drifted onto his forehead and he brushed it away. He smiled and held out his hand. "I'm Joel."

Willow narrowed her eyes as she tried to place him. He seemed so damn familiar. It took her a couple of seconds to match the name to a figure from her past. "Joel McIntyre. I remember you from school. Oh shit, Natalie is your sister!
119

Oh my God, how did I not see that earlier?"

"It's been a while since you've seen any of us. The whole clan retreating to the mountains really set us apart from people in town for a while."

"I remember that. It was after your brother disappeared. Did you ever find him?"

The light in Joel's deep brown eyes dimmed at the mention of his brother. Joel motioned for her to take a seat, waiting until she sat before he did. Cedric took the one next to her.

"Chester. Yes, we did, but he's stuck in shifter form, and has moved to the other end of the forest. We aren't sure what happened, and he isn't saying."

"If there's anything I can do, please let me know. I have a friend who is sort of engaged to the wood elf overseeing Foster's Woods. She's a faerie, and together they might be able to help. If not, maybe I can work up a spell that would bind your memories, and you could see what happened."

Joel tapped his fingers on the desk and studied her, his gaze jumping to Cedric after a second. "How come you never offered to do that?"

"Not really my realm."

Joel grunted. He turned his attention back to Willow. "Thank you, I may take you up on that, if I can get him in the same room as me. But, enough of Chester, how's it going with my partner over there? You know, he's been sweet on you since high school." The corner of Joel's mouth curved and mischief twinkled in his eyes.

Willow glanced at Cedric. She wasn't sure, but it looked like a faint blush brightened his cheeks. "He has, has he? I never would have guessed that."

"That's because he's a guy. We don't express ourselves well. Tugging pigtails and making fun of girls worked for us when we were young, and we never thought to change our approach."

"Is that why so many of you are hopelessly single?" She turned to Cedric. "And why didn't you ever tell me?"

"That I've had a thing for you since high school?" He sounded horrified at the thought.

"No. That you were part owner of this place? That's fantastic. I never would have thought you had it in you."

"I'm not sure how to take that, but no one knew. I came up with the idea and had the cash, while Joel and his family had the talent and drive. We decided to keep my involvement a secret. My reputation would have hurt more than helped."

She furrowed her brows in confusion. "I don't see what opening a restaurant has to do with your reputation of a serial dater."

"That right there. That's what people think of me. Shameless flirt who only thinks of sex and a good time." He shook his head, a self-deprecating smile on his handsome face. "We wanted a certain atmosphere and thought if people knew I was the brains behind it, it would end up being a place to hangout and hookup. Not a place to have an extraordinary meal in an upscale environment. This town has needed something like this for years. Big steaks, fresh fish, generous portions when requested."

She hummed in understanding. She was also guilty of seeing him as a man only interested in scoring with women and having a good time. Though, the last week or so, he had done a good job of showing her how different he was.

"Well, now everyone is going to know you aren't that guy anymore," she said, reaching over to squeeze his hand. "They're going to expect great things from you."

Cedric blushed a little deeper, squeezing her hand back. "As long as you're with me, that shouldn't be a problem. Come on, let's go celebrate and grab something to eat. Joel, are you going to join us?"

Joel stood and shrugged. "I've never turned down a cause for celebration."

Cedric tapped his foot impatiently as Seth and Joel occupied Willow's attention. When they finished eating, he was ready to go. He'd spent enough time sharing her with Joel, and he wanted to get Willow back to her home so he could coax sweet kisses and a hell of a lot more from her.

Joel, the good ole buddy that he was, insisted on giving her a tour of the place, to include the kitchen in which they now stood.

As soon as they stepped into the hot, bustling place, Seth made a beeline for Willow. He stuck his face in her neck and breathed in deep. She giggled like a schoolgirl and playfully batted the big man away.

"You smell nice," Seth grunted.

Her hand slid up to grab the moonstone. "That's only because I don't have kitchen smell all over me." Cedric had to wonder, again, if she even realized she did it. There was an absentmindedness to the action. "Dinner was delicious, by the way."

"Thank you." Seth grinned, big and toothy. Cedric would have been humored by the way the guy was acting since it was so out of character, but the fact he was doing it because of Willow kind of pissed him off.

"Seth was gracious enough to take over head chef duties while I ate and tended to the huge influx of customers. The bit on the restaurant turned out better than I thought. The response has been amazing. Now, I just hope we can keep it up," Joel said hopefully.

"I'm sure you will. The food is fantastic. The owners are amazing. The restaurant is in a great location. The only thing I would suggest is an outdoor dining area that opened to the woods. Maybe a giant pergola so people didn't feel like they were out in the open and vulnerable. You could put those tall outdoor heaters out there too for chilly nights. I'd go with the pyramid flame ones with the fire shooting up the middle. I know a lot of shifters would feel better sitting outside." Willow's eyes widened suddenly. "I'm so sorry, you didn't ask my opinion."

123

Cedric chuckled and wrapped his arm around her shoulder. "It's fine."

"And a great idea," Joel added. "It wouldn't take much to add it on. We could put in a door leading out without much disruption to daily operations. We should sit down soon and work that out, Ric."

Willow giggled and he squeezed her shoulder. Her amused gaze turned his way. "Now that people know you're involved, *Ric*, I'm sure they'll be clamoring to see you. I'm surprised you aren't out there now schmoozing with people. Working the crowd."

Cedric scowled at her for calling him Ric. She knew he didn't like it coming from her. He didn't get the chance to voice his opinion, though.

"That's a brilliant idea, Willow," Joel said smirking.

Cedric's plans for the evening looked grim. He knew he should be out showing his face and talking to people. He knew a lot of them had come to see if it was true, and to see if he fell on his face. But tonight was supposed to be the night. A big culmination of telling the world—okay the town—he was more than a playboy, and a private celebration with the woman he loved.

Cedric groaned. "Fine, but only for a little while. I have other plans for tonight."

They ended up spending the next four hours at the restaurant. He finally announced he had enough and escaped with Willow out the back door. She laughed the entire time he hustled her out to the SUV.

"You know it isn't nice to laugh at people," he said, pushing her up against the door.

"I'm not laughing *at* you. I'm laughing with you," she chuckled, then pinched her lips together.

"Notice, I'm not laughing. If I had known people would feel entitled to talk to me, I wouldn't have let the news come out."

She cupped a hand on the side of his face. "Oh, you poor baby. It must be hard work to have everyone want to be your friend."

He shook his head and frowned. That wasn't really the issue, and any other day he wouldn't have minded. "You know all I wanted to do was have dinner, then take you home where we could spend some time together."

"You had to know something like that would happen though. You can't announce to the world you're a respectable business owner and not think people would be curious. It's very different from the image you've put out there over the years. Playboy. Ladies man. Ne'er do well."

He pressed into her personal space, bracing his hands next to her head. "That'll teach me then." Lowering his head, he kissed her like he had been aching to do all night. He licked the seam of her mouth, sliding in when she opened for him. Their tongues tangled then retreated. He lifted his head and pressed his forehead against hers, catching his breath for a moment. "I was only concerned with one person." Soft lips met his in the briefest of dances again before he pulled back. "You."

"Oh!" She squeaked. "Why is that?" She asked, air puffing against his wet lips.

For so many reasons, but he went for his basest one. "Because I want you to know I can take care of you, of us. I want you to know there's more to me than *serial dating* and having a good time." He nipped her bottom lip, unable to resist.

"I know that," she whispered. "I've always known there was more to you, Cedric. I just didn't think you cared what I thought."

"I care a lot, love. More than I think you're willing to acknowledge." He dropped a quick, hard kiss on her mouth then got her in the SUV.

Twenty minutes and a couple of red lights later, they were back at her place. He walked her to her front door, hoping she would invite him in. He wouldn't press her for more than she was ready to give, but it didn't stop him from hoping.

"Are you coming in tonight?" She asked, as she dug her key out of the tiny purse.

Yes! "If you'd like me to," he said, struggling to keep his cool.

"I wouldn't have asked if I didn't want you to."

126

Cedric didn't need to be told twice. He wrapped his arm around her waist, scooping her up against his body at the same time as his mouth fused to hers. He felt the brush of her feet against his ankles and knew he'd lifted her off the ground.

With his free hand, he waved it over the lock, popping the door open. It bounced against the wall with a loud bang.

Willow's mouth disengaged from his. She looked over her shoulder at the door. "What the hell?"

"You have it enchanted, but it's no match for a determined warlock."

He kicked the door shut behind him and carried her off to her room.

CHAPTER ELEVEN

This is what Willow had been waiting for. Cedric didn't stop moving until he had them on her bed, him hovering over her. Their lips were still melded together. Her nails digging into his back, clinging to him tightly.

There were too many clothes between them. His suit. Her outfit. She wanted to feel his bare skin against hers. Run her hands over his chest and hips, making her way to the ass she drooled over.

Cedric was the first to get his hands on skin. His fingers danced beneath the hem of her shirt, pushing it up as he explored and caressed. She whimpered as his darker magic flowed over her. Deep, sensual need that licked and teased. Tiny currents of electricity danced in the wake of his touch, setting her body on fire. All of it made her head spin. It was a damn good thing they were on the bed.

"Damn, your skin is soft," he puffed against her lips.

"Too many clothes," she responded, frustrated that he wasn't naked. She tugged at his jacket and tried worming her hands between them.

He leaned back then reversed off the bed. He popped the button on his jacket and slid it off. He took his time folding it neatly, putting it on the chair not too far from the bed, while keeping his eyes locked onto her. It was hot as hell to see a man climb out of his suit. He rested his fingers on the top button of his vest. He had to have his clothes tailored to perfection. The vest hugged his chest nicely and tapered at his waist.

She pushed up onto her elbows, ready to take in the show. The bastard took his time popping each button. She felt like minutes ticked by before he undid the first. Then another round of waiting before the next button. There were five of those things, and when he got to the third, she'd had enough.

"*Aperta*," she said and a pointed finger at each button. They came undone one at a time without any help from him.

"Hey," he said in mock outrage, the lifting of his lips into a smile giving him away. He peeled the vest off and folded it, setting it with his jacket. Kicking off his shoes, he set them next to each other, perfectly lined up next to the chair.

"You know, I'm all for neatly folded clothes and being orderly, but you're taking entirely too long." She crawled to the end of the bed. "At this rate, I might as well go make a cup of tea and check out what's on TV. You can let me know when you're ready."

"Aren't you the impatient witch? I thought you might like a slow seduction."

"Isn't that what we've been doing for almost two weeks? Soft kisses. Tender caresses."

"I thought you liked that," he said with a mix of confusion and offense. He was too damn cute.

She got off the bed to stand in front of him. Hooking a finger between two buttons of his shirt, she jerked him forward, closing the distance between them. She got up on her tiptoes and pressed her lips to his. She devoured him, moving her mouth against his, sucking his bottom lip before letting go. "I do, but sometimes it's okay to grab what you want," she whispered, allowing the husky edge of burning desire to take hold.

He grinned and took a small step back. Waving a hand down his front; the buttons came free one by one. The shirt was tossed on top of the vest and jacket, and the pants flew next. Socks came off and he was gloriously naked.

Willow licked her lips and wondered how she didn't jump him the first day he showed up at her house under the guise of helping her.

Cedric's body was a thing of beauty. She'd always known that. Dark, sun-kissed skin was everywhere. His smooth chest, lightly furred arms and legs. Broad shoulders and ripped chest and abs filled her field of vision. Her gaze dipped, eyes rounding. She knew the man wasn't little. Had felt as much on occasion, but holy hell. Seeing his length and the width of his cock, she wondered how the man walked with such a thing when aroused.

He shifted forward, brushing his thick erection against her silk shirt. Panic tried to set in but she pushed it aside. This was her chance to see what all of the fuss was about.

"Now you're the one overdressed," he said pulling her dazed gaze. A smirk curled the corners of his mouth. His eyes had a wicked glint to them.

She was but wasn't ready to strip naked. There was something she wanted to do. Something she wanted to taste and cradle in her mouth. But first, there was a journey to take. She pressed a kiss over his heart; aware she was giving away what she felt. She flicked her tongue over his dark nipple, pulling his taste in. There was a hint of earth and storm mixed with sweat. His nipple beaded slightly, spurring her to tongue it again. She wasn't happy until she could see it tighten.

Not one to leave the other side out, she tongued and tortured his other nipple into submission before continuing her cruise down his chest. She used everything she could to explore the hard ridges of his washboard abs. Tongue. Teeth. Lips. Hands.

Focusing her energy into her hands, she let fire build beneath the surface before stroking over his sides and down to his hips. Cedric grunted and moaned as she played with his flesh. Her magic spilling from her in a bid to make him feel the intensity she did. She dropped to her knees in front of him.

Purposely ignoring the throbbing erection in front of her face, she placed soft kisses across one hip, following her trail with her hand. Switching sides, she did the same thing. Kisses and the hot slide of her magic over his skin.

His cock bobbed the closer she got to it, silently reaching out for her touch. A tortured plea left his lips as she continued to ignore his cock. His hand fell to her head, trying to push her where he wanted her.

Willow looked up his body and caught his gaze. With slow methodical movements, she wrapped her hand around the base of his dick, pushing her magic out and over it. She knew heat would seep into his skin and dance across his nerve endings.

"Fuck!"

Willow grinned when he ground the word out. She stroked him lightly, forcing a drop of pre-cum from the tip. Leaning into him, she placed her free hand on his hip and swirled her tongue around the head of his shaft. She licked away the drop with her tongue and savored the salty taste of him in her mouth. Opening her mouth, she bobbed up and down on his length. Working more and more of it in on each pass. When she had him covered in spit, she added her hand into the action. Massaging up and down, while she swirled and twirled her tongue around the head.

He was hot and smooth, his cock pulsing in her mouth. She was torn between letting him finish in her mouth or letting him fuck her silly. His hips jerked, and she was sure the decision had been made for her.

Cedric couldn't take it anymore. He needed inside of her. Needed to feel her pussy grab onto his dick as he fucked orgasm after orgasm from her. Don't get him wrong, he *loved* her lips and hand wrapped around his dick, but he had waited so long to get Willow into bed, he wasn't going to spoil his first shot.

Fuck, shot! If he didn't pull out of her mouth in the next second, he would shoot his load into her mouth. The tingling bites of magic were no help either.

On a groan, he managed to step away from Willow and that damn talented mouth of hers. He helped her up off the ground and immediately stripped her of her clothes. Underneath the silk blouse was a cream-colored lace bra, and she wore matching lace bikini panties. His mouth watered at the sight and his brain shut down. He was sure he was standing there with his mouth open and drool coming out.

"Cedric?" He heard her whisper, uncertainly clouding her voice.

Her words from earlier echoed in his ears. *Sometimes it's okay to grab what you want.* Damn, he wanted her. "Décrocher," he said, unhooking her bra with that one little command.

She gasped, and he leered as her bra fell away, revealing her beautiful breasts. They were perfect creamy globes with

134

dark pink tips. The exact shade of the flowers on her tattoo. He wanted to spend his time learning her body, but he needed her too much. His erection throbbed and his balls ached.

He shoved her panties down her legs before backing her up against the bed. She tumbled backwards. He followed her down. As if it was the most natural thing, her legs parted, cradling his hips. The feel of her legs around him, damn near undid him. For so long this was what he wanted. He thrust against her mound, unable to resist. Loving the feel of the neatly trimmed tuft of hair abrade his shaft.

He kissed her hard, pouring as much feeling and passion into it. He shifted his hips and reached between them, aligning his cock up to her wet entrance. He pushed forward, forcing her slick folds to part, allowing him entry. He didn't stop until he was buried deep inside, his balls resting against her ass.

God, it was going to be quick. Wet heat surrounded him, and the small, minute spasms of her core rippled over his shaft. His eyes rolled into to back of his head at the exquisite feel.

Willow moaned low in her throat. Pleasure washed over her face, her mouth dropping open. Her legs came around his hips, locking them together. He didn't know if she thought he would leave or if she wanted him to wait.

"Please, Cedric," she begged.

Those two little words destroyed his control. She never begged...for anything. Snapping his hips back, he thrust hard and deep. Angling his strokes so he was riding her clit. Over and over again he pounded into her.

Sweat slicked his body as tension gathered at the base of his spine. There would be no holding it off any longer. He fucked her harder, each bump of his pelvis against her clit pulling a gasp from her lips.

He felt her magic build and shimmer around them, calling to his in a way he'd never felt before. There was a crack of thunder as he moved faster, getting lost in the feel of finally being with Willow. It was everything he dreamed it would be...and more.

Willow's pussy suddenly tightened around him, clamping down on his cock. Her head tipped back as her body arched into him, a scream leaving her lips and echoing through the room. Her magic seemed to snap, and they were engulfed with flames.

It was too much and triggered his orgasm. He slammed into her again and let go, a roar ripping from his throat. The pressure in his spine released as he pumped cum into her. His magic erupted into the frenzy. Lightning sparked around them, merging with the fire. It was a damn good thing they couldn't be hurt by it all.

Minutes passed before he collapsed next to her. He arranged her so her back was to him; her ass snuggled against his groin. Her head rested on his arm. Breathing the scent of sex and Willow in, peace filled him. He tried to resist it, but his eyes slammed shut.

Hours later Cedric woke up. Willow was snuggled

against him in the same position they had fallen asleep in. Moonlight seeped through the window giving him just enough light to see the tattoo on her back. He traced over her shoulder, following the thick tree limb down onto her back.

Shifting slightly so he could get a better look he continued his journey over the ink. The tree limb connected to the trunk. It curved sharply and he wondered what it meant. What thing in her life had that drastic of a turn?

"High school," she mumbled, starling him.

"How did you know I was wondering about it?"

"I know you, Cedric. You pay attention and like to know how people tick. It was natural to assume you remembered me telling you it represented my life, the twists and turns. High school wasn't a great time but when we graduated I resolved to change a few things. Mostly how people perceived me." She rolled to face him, brushing a kiss across his lips. "Now go back to sleep."

He wasn't ready to though. He kissed her, running his lips over her jaw and down her arched neck. Her breath caught in her throat he couldn't resist pushing her onto her back and making love to her again.

When they were finished, he collapsed with her pressed into his side and they both drifted to sleep.

CHAPTER TWELVE

Jun 16th – Tuesday

Strolling through the field, Willow felt like a queen. She had a hot man on her arm that made her head spin, and the confidence that went with it, at least on the outside. She had always wondered what it would feel like to be the one with him. Receive the jealous looks from other women, and a few men. Granted, some of those looks held a bit more than the green-eyed monster. There was pure hatred and possibly vengeance, but she chose to ignore those spiteful bitches. Because being with Cedric felt wonderful, she was happy and maybe even loved.

There was a part of her that refused to believe what their relationship turned into, if she could even define it. He was no longer her nemesis, the boy who taunted and teased her through the years. He was the man she looked forward to seeing every day. The one she found her thoughts drifting to when he was away. The man in her dreams when she closed her eyes at night, all while missing him by her side.

The moonstone around her neck pulsed with steady heat. She was convinced more than ever it responded to Cedric, but she also wondered if it was the only reason he was with her. His change of heart when it came to her was… abrupt. At least that was how it seemed to her.

Cedric squeezed her hand, grabbing her attention. He leaned down and kissed her, sending a flutter through her belly. That light, butterfly kiss made her want to forget making an appearance. All her thoughts centered on heading to her place and crawling back in bed with him.

Who would have known she'd turn into a nymph? How she would need him every moment of the day. She chuckled lightly, drawing a raised eyebrow from him. She shook her head, "It's nothing."

He snorted, "I doubt that."

They stopped in front of the Transfiguration demonstration. Other witches and warlocks milled around, waiting to see what would happen. The skill to perform the magic to change something from an object to a creature or a creature to a human was high. Not many in the coven had it.

There were some not-so strict rules on transfiguration magic. The community at large frowned upon people doing it in the hopes of disguising their features or changing in order to deceive. Teenage girls practiced the art in order to enhance their features to entice the boys they liked. Teenage boys did it to look better or bigger than they really were.

Typical events most got over once it backfired in their faces. But progressing into adulthood, it was considered a bit more taboo. The only ones allowed to alter someone else's image were witches and warlocks working for law enforcement.

Hazel, the witch Willow worked with on the planning committee stepped up and pulled a black velvet curtain aside to reveal different objects: A cup, a bowl, a bird, and a rabbit. The basic items all of them had worked with at one time or another when learning the different aspects of their craft.

She started her spiel, explaining what she was going to do to each item, then one by one transformed them into something different. The cup turned into a bowl. The bowl into a bucket. Simple things for simple tasks. When a man joined her, a large warlock with long black hair and dark piercing eyes, the women in the crowd perked up and pushed forward.

He scanned the crowd, and when his eyes landed on Willow, she couldn't help but fidget in place. Cedric looked down at her, and she knew he was wondering what her problem was.

She really didn't have an answer. There was something about him; a familiarity, but she didn't know him. Had never seen him before. The man's gaze turned fierce, his eyes narrowed and a glimmer of vibrant purple sparked in them. Her head reeled when her first thought was of Edward, her familiar. It couldn't be him, could it? She left him at home curled up on the back of the couch.

The man moved over to Hazel and whispered in her ear

before stepping into the crowd. He made his way toward Willow, the people around them parting before he even got close to pushing his way through.

The hairs on the back of her neck stood on end, goosebumps skittered across her skin. The mysterious man stopped in front of them and looked at Cedric, then to Willow. He reached out and touched the stone around her neck. Ice shot through her, chilling her to the bone.

She stepped back on a gasp, her hand coming out of Cedric's. He turned toward her, brows furrowed and confused. "What the hell is going on?" He asked, and turned back toward the man.

"She is wearing a moonstone," the man rumbled. His deep voice vibrated through her body and shook the ground beneath her feet.

Cedric stepped in front of her in a protective manner. "What of it?"

"You know she is looking for love? Someone to spend the rest of eternity with?"

Cedric nodded sharply. His body tensed, instinct told her to step forward to rest her hand on his back. "I know what she's looking for," Cedric said, a thread of steel weaving though his voice.

"And you think you can give it to her?" The man chuckled low and deadly. People moved away from him.

She peeked around Cedric's body to see the man's eyes

light up with the vibrant purple again, this time consuming his irises. Sparks of electricity crackled from his hands.

"I can give her everything she's ever wanted. I *am* everything she's ever wanted." Cedric's hands balled into fists and began to glow. The spheres of lights grew brighter and brighter, creeping up his arms. She knew his main power was current and lightning.

The man wasn't intimidated in the least by the show of power. He cocked his head, narrowing his gaze. "When you touch her, what do you feel? Does fire burst through your veins? Does the moonstone glow?"

"It doesn't matter what I feel," Cedric replied.

"When I touched her, it was like ice, shards of pain and cold enough to freeze a person's heart. She is not meant for me."

"You were never an option."

A slight smile curled the man's lips. "But that isn't what you thought the first time we met."

Willow stepped out from behind Cedric, intent on confronting the man. She'd never seen him before, and she didn't think Cedric had either. He appeared as wary as she was. "Whoa there."

Cedric stuck his arm out, holding her back. Willow wanted to walk up to the man and look directly into his eyes. See for herself if he was telling the truth.

"The first time we met? I've never seen you before in my life," Cedric said, confirming what she thought. He curved his hand around her hip and pulled her closer to him.

Her body brushed up against his, setting the moonstone on fire. She moaned softly as wisps of sensual heat licked over her skin.

One of the man's dark eyebrows rose, and Cedric turned his head in her direction. He looked to be as shocked as she felt that the sound escaped. A slow blush heated her cheeks, and she resisted covering them, aware she would draw more attention that way.

"Heat. She feels heat whisk through her blood at your touch. The kind only a lover can produce." The man's grin grew wide. "That is as it should be." He turned abruptly and headed back to Hazel. As he walked toward her, his body morphed, twisting and reshaping gracefully into a black cat.

Willow's mouth dropped open. "Holy shit! It *is* Edward."

The cat cast a glance in her direction and flicked its tail. He vaulted into Hazel's arms, to the surprise of everyone around them. His deep rumbling purr could be heard from a distance.

The crowd around them started to clap. Hazel curtsied and pulled the velvet curtain back down, disappearing before Willow's brain processed what the hell had just happened.

"How about we go home?" Cedric asked, draping an

arm over her shoulders.

"Yeah, I think I've had enough fun tonight."

They walked away, heading back to where Cedric's SUV was parked. Her mind was too full to really get a handle on what that little show was about. Had her cat really been a man? Did he give his approval of Cedric? Was he even coming home? The questions came one right after another. More followed.

"That was one hell of a transfiguration demonstration," Cedric quipped.

It was the perfect thing for him to say. She laughed and relaxed into him.

Cedric got Willow home and stripped her of her jeans and shirt. He left her lacy panties and matching bra on; loving the way it looked against her skin. And the way it abraded his. Though, that wasn't what he had in mind at the moment.

"Don't move or speak unless I tell you," he rumbled next to her ear. He wanted her standing at the end of the bed, facing away from him. He kneaded her stiff shoulders. Ran his thumbs down her neck. Inch by inch, he made his way down her body, her body relaxing into his ministrations. Firm hands and light kisses. With a flick of the wrist, her bra came undone. He pushed the straps off her shoulders, and ran his hands under her arms, peeling the lace from her breasts. The garment dropped to the floor in front of her.

Cupping her breasts with his hands, he lifted them, squeezed them, and pinched her nipples. A soft moan escaped the back of her throat full of needy arousal and want. Flicking his nails over the buds, he didn't stop until they tightened. She squirmed and shifted from foot to foot.

He leaned in and nipped her neck. "Uh, uh, uh. Good girls know to stand still like they were told. That's the only way they'll get more. You're a good girl, aren't you, Willow?"

"Yes," she whispered.

His cock jumped in his jeans, making him wince in pain. His whole reason for keeping the damn things on was because Willow had had a bit of a shock at the celebration, and he wasn't quite sure what was going through her mind. He could barely wrap his head around the fact that her familiar wasn't a familiar after all. A small part of him wondered if the cat had been able to transfigure all along, or if it was because Cedric allowed him to siphon power from him. Or, maybe it was because Cedric and Willow were meant to be, and now that they were together, he was no longer needed. Too many questions with no answers in the foreseeable future. There would be time to figure that out later. Right now, he wanted to concentrate on the woman in front of him.

Sliding his hands down her sides and up her back, he massaged her tight muscles. As he got lower, her breathing picked up. When he reached the small of her back, he knelt behind her. He slid his thumbs under the waistband of her panties, gliding them back and forth. Lower and lower. He worked his way to the sides, hooking his thumbs and dragging them down her legs. He showered kisses over her buttocks, down her firm, rounded skin, and nipped the bottom where it met her thigh.

She squeaked but stayed her ground.

"Step," he instructed, pulling the panties off one foot then the other, dropping them on top of the forgotten bra.

Skimming back up her legs with his hands, he stood, skating his hands over her ass, and then pressed on the small of her back, pushing her forward. "Put your hands on the end of the bed. Spread your legs."

She adjusted her stance and popped up on her tiptoes.

"Damn, you're beautiful." He grabbed her by the hips and stepped up behind her, grinding his rigid jean-covered cock against he naked pussy. Fuck, it felt good. The rough fabric doing a number on both of them. Willow's head dropped lower as she pushed back against him. She rocked in tiny increments up and down his length. If he wasn't so intent on making it all about Willow relaxing, he would unzip his pants, whip out his dick, and ram into her in one thrust. Quick, hard, and deep. He wouldn't stop fucking her until he came inside. Shoving in as far as he could get.

Forcing himself to take a step back, he dropped to his knees. Every inch of her pretty pink pussy was on display. He breathed in deep, allowing her sweet arousal to fill his lungs. Damn, her lust was intoxicating. He was driven to taste her. To feast on her flesh and drink her in.

He licked her slit from one end to the other. Swirling his

tongue into her opening. He fucked her with it, then started all over again. Lick. Fuck. Lick. Fuck.

She whimpered and her legs began to shake. Finding her nub with his tongue he concentrated on it. Tonguing it. Sucking it. Then doing it again and again. She was getting close to coming and he wanted to feel the first fall. Easing one finger inside, he thrust it in and out. She started pumping her hips, taking more and more of his digit. Her moans and whimpers turned to grunts and mewls. Adding a second digit, he increased the thrust and clamped his lips around her clit, sucking it hard.

She cried out, her pussy rippling and convulsing against his fingers. The muscles locked down in a bid to keep him embedded inside her.

Fuck, it was an overwhelming feeling.

He stood and ran a hand over her ass, pressing down on her lower back. He wanted her to stay in that position. With his other hand, he undid his jeans and zipper, shoving the pants down as far as he could.

His cock bobbed, and the feeling of freedom had his balls tingling. He pumped his dick a couple times, a bead of pre-cum escaping the tip. He guided it to her wet entrance, circling the outside with the head, lubing it slightly. He pushed in and she pushed back. He slid in deeper, basking in the excruciating slowness of their joining. The tight walls of her pussy sucking him in.

Pulling back, she whimpered and tried to follow. He gripped her hips and held her still. A grin curved his mouth.

He wasn't going anywhere. With just the head of his cock inside, he took a calming breath and thrust all the way in. Willow cried out with pleasure and then he was moving. Thrusting in and out, over and over again.

They worked together, their speed picking up. Her cries echoing throughout the room. He hunched over her, sliding his hands from her waist to her shoulders. He curled his fingers, gripping her hard and probably leaving bruises, but he was too far-gone to adjust.

"Fuck, yeah, Willow." He grunted, slamming his hips against her. "Take all I've got, love."

He was holding her up at this point, her hands no longer on the bed frame. He felt her hand between her legs. Stroking his dick for a second as it slid in and out. She rubbed her clit, and it didn't take long for her to come. She threw her head back screaming his name and he tumbled right after.

Fingers locked onto her shoulder, he thrust into her one last time. The force of his orgasm shaking his legs and pulling his balls tight against his body. His energy drained from him in a heartbeat and his dick softened, slipping from her body.

Cedric tapped her lightly on the ass. "Go lay down."

He stepped out of his jeans, leaving them in a pile at the end of the bed, then crawled up next to her, flopping onto his back out of breath. Willow curled into his side, resting her head on his shoulder. Her arm draped over his chest. Her fingers made patterns on his skin, sending a torrent of ridiculously happy feelings through him. He loved the fact she was a snuggler, even though he'd never been a fan of it before. Being with Willow wasn't like anything he'd experienced ever before, but he knew it wouldn't be.

She was his heart and soul. He could be himself around her and not that douche-bag guy everyone saw him as. He was able to show her who he really was. That he'd grown up and was finally ready to love her like she deserved.

She hummed and burrowed a little deeper after he managed to get the covers out from under them. Cool sheets covered them and almost every ounce of stress drained from his body. There was one thing keeping him from complete and total bliss.

"Is that a happy hum?" He asked into the quiet of the room.

"Uh huh." She replied sleepily.

In the darkness, the soft glow of her moonstone started to grow brighter. Reaching over, he plucked it off her chest and felt the warmth begin to radiate down his fingers.

"Love?"

"Hmmm..."

"Why don't you take this off?" He tugged lightly on the necklace she had been wearing around her neck for the past two weeks. He knew she hadn't taken it off at any point, and he was more than ready for her to set it aside. She didn't need it to see that he was in love with her. He'd told her and shown her in so many ways.

"Not until the solstice is over," she mumbled.

"But you don't need it. I think we've proven that."

"Fantastic sex doesn't automatically mean love of a lifetime," she said, sounding not quite as sleepy anymore.

A part of him, his ego specifically, did a high-five at the fantastic sex comment. The other part of him wondered what else she needed to believe he was the one she was meant to be with.

She shifted away slightly and tilted her head up. A loud snap sounded in the room. Fireflies appeared out of thin air casting dim light throughout the room, enough to where they could see each other.

"In this case it does though," he said, shoving to sit up against the headboard.

Willow followed suit, putting even more distance between them. She pulled the sheet to cover her breasts. "You don't know that for sure."

"Yes, I do. I told you the first day I came over that I loved you. We are meant for each other, Willow. Have been since we were five. And if you don't believe that, then you need to listen to the moonstone. It heats to my touch. It reacts only to me. If you believe in Aphrodite and the gift she has bestowed upon you, you have to believe that I'm your fated mate."

"Why? Because you showed up the day after my rite to the Goddess?"

Cedric had to think about that one for a moment. Saying yes would prove her point that they were together because of the moonstone, and she might never take it off. Saying no would mean explaining himself and trying to convince her he was sincere.

"You don't even know what to say, do you?" Her lips thinned and a flicker of hurt drifted into her eyes.

"I do, but either way I have a fight on my hands. If I say yes, then you'll believe I'm only here because of the moonstone and the rite. If I say no, then I have to explain how I planned on coming to your house to begin with and hope you believe me."

She snorted and crossed her arms over her chest.

He wasn't a fan of the derision in that sound. "Who do you think got rid of Perry in order to replace him? That didn't happen on a whim. I fixed him up with someone I knew he couldn't resist and was there to ensure I was the man assigned to help you. I've been planning on finding a way back into your life after the royal fuck-up of a date. I missed you, Wills."

Her eyes narrowed and there was a spark of distrust glittering in them. "You expect me to believe that?"

"You're damn right I do." He reached out and ran his fingers over the branches of her tattoo. "This tree that represents your family and is about you, the twists and dead-ends in your relationships. The deep, sudden turn leading to a new branch in your life. I hate to break it to you, but that's us. Our fights and making up. The years when we didn't talk or barely looked at each other. It's time for the next step. A more intimate, caring step."

"So, what you're saying is that your plan was to seduce me and get me into bed to bring it to an *intimate* level."

He laughed out loud. Long and hearty. "Oh, love, if my plan was to seduce you, I would have done so the first day. As egotistical as it may be, I've known you've had feelings for me for years. At any time I could have taken advantage of that, but I didn't. And, do you want to know why?"

Willow shook her head. "No, I don't."

"I'm going to tell you anyway. Because I knew you would fall in love with me, and I wasn't ready for that kind of commitment. I wasn't mature enough to handle it. I am now. I'm ready for everything you'll give me. Time. The pleasure of your presence. Your love. I want it all, and we can't have that while you're still wearing that necklace. You will never believe my declarations of love otherwise."

"You're right I won't, and I'm not taking it off until after the solstice is over. It's what I promised myself in order to give my deepest wish a chance."

Cedric clenched his jaw to keep from saying something he shouldn't. He also clenched his hands to keep from ripping that damn necklace off. She needed to see for herself that what he said was true. They were meant to be. Their lives intertwined from the age of five. That beautiful tattoo on her body represented *them*. *Their* journey. Whether she would ever admit that, he didn't know.

Sucking in a huge breath, he climbed from the bed and pulled on his clothes. Willow sat on the bed; her eyes round with surprise. His heart ached with what he was about to do. But she needed to see that she needed him. Missed him. Goddamn, fucking loved him.

"This isn't how I wanted the evening to end, I never planned on leaving your side, but I can't stay here with you while you put more faith in that necklace than you do me. I'm here because I want to be, not because of Aphrodite or your moonstone."

CHAPTER THIRTEEN

Jun 20th – Saturday

Willow strolled through the fields like she had done three days ago with Cedric, but it felt wrong. The fair-like booths, the sights, sounds and smells, the people milling about were all the same, but they didn't hold the same appeal as before.

Nothing did actually now that Cedric was gone. A pang shot through her heart damn near crippling her. She reached for the necklace before she remembered she had taken it off. Never realizing how much of a crutch it had become in such a short time. Allowing her to use the excuse that it was the moonstone that brought him to her and never really letting her heart believe he wanted her of his own free will.

It didn't take long to figure out the one thing she desired most in the entire universe—Cedric. But she managed to screw that up with little to no effort on her part. He had asked for one simple thing, for her to take the necklace off. He swore on his life his affection was solely his own. Aphrodite and the moonstone weren't the causes of his interest, even though he had shown up the day after her rite.

She believed him…now. She didn't quite know how to fix it though.

Sure, she could show up at his place, but then she'd have to contend with his heartbroken brother. And considering she *may* have broken his brother's heart, there would be hell to pay. Or, lots of yelling and woman-bashing.

And, if you loved Cedric, which you do, then you'd put up with it. She would too. She needed to stop hesitating when it came to him. Stop questioning how he felt and take a chance. If, in the end, her heart ended up getting broken, then at least she had what she'd always wanted with the man.

She needed to find him…now. Willow stopped walking and finally took a look around. She had ended up in front of the one place she didn't want to be, Magical Binding. She knew from reading the proposal that it was more than learning spells that restrained someone metaphysically, preventing them from doing something such as causing harm to themselves or others. That was for the daytime crowd.

At night, Magical Binding turned to sexual delights. The use of magic to bind a partner, limiting the use of their hands and legs, much like hooks and cuffs in the BDSM community.

Her cousin Autumn stood in front of her husband, who she had pressed up against a makeshift wall. Her hand was on his bare chest. He had on leather pants and a big ass grin—nothing else.

"Tonight I'm going to demonstrate how to bind your partner for your pleasure," Autumn began. "It really is a simple spell, but you need to take care. Done in anger and haste, your partner will be able to break the spell. Magic in order to hurt another is wrong." She turned to the crowd gathering about her. Brushing the straight black mane of hair off her shoulder, she gave them a cheeky grin. "But then, you all know that."

There was laughter and snickers from the crowd. Everyone knew not to use magic on others of their own kind. But what Magic Regulators didn't know, certainly didn't hurt them.

"My volunteer, Ivan, who is also my husband, knows I do everything out of love. Hell, he even asks for it." Autumn smoothed her hand up his chest then down his right arm. Circling his wrist with her fingers, she drew his arm up, pressed the back of his hand next to his head. "Like the majority of my family, my spells and incantations are done in Latin. You may do them in whatever language you prefer, but for the purpose of this demonstration, I will say it in Latin and repeat the phrase for you in English."

"Ligaveris manu...bind hand." A spark of blue popped around Ivan's wrist. Autumn let go and repeated the same action and words on the other side. She stepped to the side, but didn't go far. "If someone would like to check to see that his hands are, indeed, locked into place, please?"

Someone pushed through the crowd amid grunts and murmurs. The hairs on the back of Willow's neck stood on end. Cedric stepped to the front and joined her cousin. "I will," he said, the deep timber of his voice tripping down Willow's spine.

Her breath caught in her throat at the sight of him. His beautiful brown locks were no longer down to his shoulders. It was cut into a stylish, professional haircut befitting the businessman he was. Tapered sides with a little length on top. It was parted on one side and combed back. It made him look like less of a rogue, but not too much. The new hairstyle went well with his look. Expensive looking, well-fitting jeans with artfully placed holes, the black shiny shoes, and long sleeve collared polo with silk accents around the wrists.

She was rooted to her spot, unable to turn and dash away. This was not the place she wanted to talk to him, beg him to forgive her and take her back. Before her brain could reconnect with her legs, Cedric turned to the crowd, his gaze landing on her.

That wicked smile, that curve of the left side of his mouth appeared, and a predatory glint shone in his eyes. Keeping his eyes on Willow, he tugged Ivan's hands, one after the other. "It's perfect," he said, but she didn't think he was talking about the binding.

"As I said it would be," Autumn smiled. "As simple as it was to do, it is just as simple to undo." She placed her fingers around Ivan's wrist. "Véndi manu." Blue sparks appeared and disappeared as she undid her husband's hands. Ivan stepped away from the wall and dropped a kiss on his wife's lips.

158

There was light applause from the crowd, and Willow desperately hoped the show was over.

"Now, if someone from the audience would like to try it before we move on to other more…entertaining forms of binding."

"I will," Cedric spoke before Autumn had finished.

A mischievous smile curled her cousin's lips. "Of course, Cedric. And who would you like to practice on?"

Gemma stepped forward from the front row, a couple people to Willow's left. She hadn't noticed the woman before. "Oh, I'll be Cedric's volunteer," she purred. "For *anything* he wants to do."

"Like hell," Willow murmured and made a beeline for him without thinking of the repercussions. "Sorry, Gemma, but he's already taken." She turned and put her back to the wall, realizing what she had just done. Her heart took flight in her chest and nausea churned her stomach.

Cedric moved in front of her, looking down into her panicked face. "It's about damn time," he said. Blocking the crowd's view of them with his body, he grabbed her hand and pinned it next to her head. "Main bind." Silver and white flashes of magic sparked in the air. A phantom pressure held her hand in place. Sliding his big hand down her left arm, he did the same thing, except after her hand was bound in place; he lowered his head and kissed her.

His hands came up to cup her face gently, thumbs smoothing over her cheeks. He teased her, coaxed her into

159

kissing him back. It wasn't such a hardship to do. Before the kiss could get deeper, more intimate, he pulled away and stepped to the side.

"Let's test to see how well you did, because we all know the kiss was spot on," Autumn said with a smirk, then tugged on Willow's arms. "Very good. Now, is there something you want to do before you unbind her?"

Cedric looked at the raven-haired witch. "As a matter of fact, there is. Willow and I have a few things to work out."

Autumn grinned and stepped back into her husband's arms. Cedric knew a moment's jealousy as he observed the couple. He wanted that ease and familiarity with Willow, and he was going to get it. There was one day left in the solstice celebration, and he would have her commitment to him come hell or high water.

"I am to assume to bind your lover's legs, it's the same principle?"

Autumn nodded. "Of course. I would use ankle as the term though. Binding the leg can make them immoveable."

Cedric crouched quickly and placed his hands on Willow's ankles. "Chevilles bind." The now familiar sparks of magic glinted in the air before puffing out.

He stood and studied the woman he was madly in love with. He had missed her for three damn days. Moped around his apartment. Listened to his brother curse women and the ground they walked on. He had also done a little soul searching and made some personal changes. He wanted Willow to see him differently. And she had, but not fully.

He felt her eyes on him. "You once asked me when would I grow up."

"And I recall saying I didn't want to know." She pinched her lips together as soon as the words left her mouth.

He didn't think she meant to be snarky, but she also couldn't help it. "Now love, you shouldn't tell lies to the man who can set you free."

Willow shrugged and tipped her head in Autumn's direction. "She can undo the spell."

Autumn sighed dramatically. "Sorry, cuz. He did it in French. You know how terrible I am with that. There's a chance I'll mispronounce something and you'll end up a frog."

Willow frowned. "Some help you are. And to think I introduced you to Ivan after my terrible blind date with him."

"And I am forever grateful, and that's why I'm giving Cedric his moment with you. You're stubborn, and I know you love him." Autumn turned her attention to him. "Want me to do a magical barrier so you can have alone time with her?"

"Thank you, but no. I want everyone to know how I feel about her and how she feels about me." He turned to the crowd. "You see, I'm in love with Willow and have been for years."

"Yeah, right," a woman snorted in disbelief. It was Gemma.

"Yes, that is right. My life has been intertwined with Willow since I was a child. We were always meant to be. But because I can be an ass, she had no cause to believe me when I showed up out of the blue declaring my love. It also didn't help that she paid tribute to Aphrodite, and the Goddess gifted Willow with her deepest wish. When I showed up the following day, Willow got it in her fool head that I was only there because of the moonstone she wears around her neck."

"What moonstone?" Someone in the crowd asked.

Cedric frowned. Was the man blind? He turned to point to the necklace. "Where the fuck is it?"

"I took it off," Willow replied.

Cedric's gaze jumped to hers. "You what? When?" His pulse picked up as excitement coursed through his chest. Could she finally believe in him?

"I took it off the day after you left. You were right. I didn't need it. I was using it to keep from letting my heart fully believe you loved me. I figured if I wore it you wouldn't leave. I thought the moment I took it off, you'd come to your senses and my heart would shatter into a million pieces."

"I told you that wouldn't happen."

"I know and it took you leaving and my heart aching before it sunk in. I should have had faith in you and I didn't. I'm sorry."

Cedric didn't know what to say, but he did know what he wanted to hear. "And…"

"And I love you. I've always loved you, ever since that time I punched you in the nose."

He stood there staring at her, his mind filled with too many things he wanted to do. Kiss her. Drag her home. Make love to her. It really didn't matter where and if he could get away with it, he'd keep her bound to the wall and fuck her into submission with her screaming her love for him.

He knelt quickly. "Délier chevilles." Standing he grabbed her wrists. "Délier les mains." Before the magic dissipated, he wrapped his arms around her. "Maison." They vanished before everyone's eyes and landed back at Willow's home.

"You're mine now, love." He said, his lips crashing down on hers. He navigated them to her bedroom and, by sheer force of will, managed not to rip her clothes as he divested them from her body.

"I've always been yours," she panted. Her slim hand wedged between their bodies popping the button of his jeans and shoving them down. He pulled his shirt over his head, and within seconds they were on the bed.

She giggled and ran her hands through his hair. "I like the new look."

"And I like you." He spent the rest of the night proving to her how much.

EPILOGUE

Willow and Cedric stood in front of the bonfire, Cedric's arms wrapped around the woman's shoulders from behind. Chloe could see the love shining in Willow's eyes as she looked up over her shoulder at Cedric. The warlock looked down at her with an intensity that almost knocked Chloe back. The randy warlock seemed to have given up his ways and claimed the quiet witch.

"They appear to be in love," Chloe's companion said.

She glanced at the statuesque woman out of the corner of her eye. "They do."

Aphrodite brushed her long, golden-red hair off her shoulder, a smug expression on her face.

"You seem quite pleased with yourself," Chloe

commented, fully turning her attention to the Goddess next to her.

"I am. The moonstone and the blessing I gave the witch brought her exactly what she wanted. I love it when a plan comes together." Aphrodite turned from the bonfire and the couple they had come to spy on. There was a twinkle of mischief sparkling in her eyes as she looked around. Witches and Warlocks were all around, spilling magic and sexual vibes everywhere the eye turned. "What shall we do now? I feel like playing with the creatures here. Sipping some of the magic they hold." She zeroed in on a large warlock with long black hair and massive shoulders. He stood well above the crowd, with an air of ancient superiority around him.

"He is a lovely creature," Chloe said, acknowledging the woman's choice in companion. "I'm sure he will please you greatly. I will be heading back to Olympus, though. I have a meeting with your son tomorrow, and I need to be at my best. He is more challenging than I thought he would be."

"He can be. Others think he is soft because of what he does. They miss the intelligence that goes with his gift." Keen eyes focused on Chloe. "You are enjoying your game with Eros."

Chloe tilted her head up marginally. "Yes. He has made this year…interesting. I think when it is all over, I will enjoy him even more."

Aphrodite threw her head back and laughed, husky and low. It had a sexual allure to it that rolled over the skin and aroused all that heard it. She wasn't called the Goddess of love, beauty, and sexual rapture for nothing. "I'm sure you will; but remember, Eros is not meant to be yours forever."

Chloe snorted. She already knew that. "I'm well aware of that. One month is all I want. Anything beyond that is negotiable."

The massive warlock Aphrodite scoped out earlier appeared next to them. He dipped his head and held out his hand. She smiled and placed her hand into his. "Tell my son I said hello."

"Of course." Wrapping the black cloak she wore tighter around her body, she faded into thin air. Reappearing in her own realm, in her room. Disrobing, she hung her garments and crawled into bed. "Until tomorrow, Eros," she whispered and allowed slumber to pull her under.

THE END

WILLOW'S INVOCATION
TO APHRODITE

In the name of Aphrodite, (She lit the first candle)
Goddess of love, (She lit the second candle)
Beauty, (She lit the third candle)
And Fertility, (She lit the last candle)
I invoke thee. (She flicked her fingers and the flame went
out)
Bless this stone and all it represents.
Help it bring to me my one true desire.
The love of my life.
The light of my soul.
The man who completes me,
Makes me whole.
In the name of Aphrodite,
Goddess of love, (She blew out the first candle, going in the
opposite direction)
Beauty, (She blew out the second candle)
And fertility, (She blew out the third candle)
As I will it, it shall be so! (She blew out the final candle)

FOREIGN LANGUAGE PHRASES

French
Pain et du Chocolat - Bread & Chocolate
Main bind – Bind hand
Chevilles bind –Bind ankles
Délier chevilles – Unbind ankles
Délier les mains – Unbind hands
Maison - Home

Latin
Ignis - Fire
Aperta – Open
Ligaveris manu – Bind hand
Véndi manu – Unbind hand

Thane: January
Mystic Zodiac, Book 1

Fallen Angel Thane has been exiled to the realm of humans and Mystics for almost fifty years after what he considers a slight *misunderstanding*, too bad Zeus didn't agree. After the blush of exile wears off, Thane dedicates his new life to helping those in need, all in the hope of impressing the imposing God.

A visit from his Watcher with one more task sets Thane up to finally get what he's dreamed about for decades… his rightful place back on Olympus with his brothers. All he needs to do is keep one woman from "doing something stupid." He determined to ignore his body responding for the first time in almost fifty years in order to go home.

Amara Hope is desperate to bring her brother home, traveling into the heart of Viral City day after day putting her life at risk. As her last living relative, he's all she has left. When a hunky Good Samaritan grudgingly offers help, she's all too willing to accept. Once they get her brother home and begin spending more time together, the more Amara knows he's the one for her.

What the two don't know is that the Gods are playing games with their lives, and they're on a collision course with love.

Word Count: 32,299

Parvati: February
Mystic Zodiac, Book 2

Parvati Shiva, a true descendent of the Goddess of love and devotion, is fed up. She runs a successful dating site, connecting Mystics and humans all over the world with their one true love. The only she hasn't been able to find love for is…her.

When a hacker gets into her network and website, shutting down her site in the height of the busy season, she calls on her cousin Jag for help, who in turn reaches out to an old friend.

Colin Patterson, IT guru and confirmed bachelor, quickly agrees to help his friend's sister out with her computer problem, hoping it will be a long drawn out process. He's eager to escape his mother's matchmaking Valentine's Day party. She's invited all of the single women—and a few men—to jump-start his dating life, something he has no interest in at all.

One mistaken identity later, Colin ruins his chance with the beautiful Indian woman he's instantly attracted to. Will he be able to prove he isn't a boss bashing idiot, save Parvati's company, and win her affections before he doesn't have a reason to stick around?

Warning: This book contains a geeky hero who can't keep his mouth shut, a strong willed businesswoman dealing in love, and an attraction that neither can deny. ***Please note:* This book has a hot M/M scene.**
Word Count: 26,817

Gideon: March
Mystic Zodiac, Book 3

Gideon Deckard is finally getting a little time away from the Keystone Predator Pack to go wolf. All he has planned is a week of running wild through the Grand Canyon before the hiking season starts back up. Once it does, he'll go back to what he does best...being the Alpha he was born to be.

Ryder Sparks can barely contain her excitement. She's taking a week off from work at the family store, Sparks Sporting & Outdoors, and going on her dream vacation. A four-day hiking trip on a lesser traveled trek through the Grand Canyon. The season has opened early and she was the first to get the coveted pass. She's looking forward to pushing herself on her first solo trip and discovering who she was really meant to be.

A run in with a massive grey wolf has Ryder stumbling and getting knocked out. When she wakes up, she's back in her tent and there's a hunky man there to help her get back on her feet. When she finds out he's a wolf-shifter instead of freaking out, she decides to go on the adventure of a lifetime with him. Now all she has to do is convince Gideon to give her a chance to be his one and only Luna.

Word Count: 36,270

Lisa: April
Mystic Zodiac, Book 4

For three years Lisa Cannon has been at Jack Morgan's every beck and call. As his executive personal assistant it's in the job description, except she's beginning to think she's gone above and beyond the call of duty. She hasn't had time off in so long she's pretty sure her nymph side is dying a slow death inside. After arranging for a week away, she's set to feed her nymph with every sexual fantasy that comes to mind. If they happen to all revolve around the man who keeps her tied to her desk, that's all for the better.

Jack knows he shouldn't do it but does anyway. He cancels his assistant's vacation…again. He can't stand the thought of her unleashing her nymph side on anyone but him. Over the past three years he's slowly fallen in love with the petite beauty that keeps his personal and professional life running smoothly.

When Lisa goes on vacation anyway, Jack knows there's only one thing to do. He needs to find a way into the Mystic-only club and claim the woman who has stolen his heart.

Word Count: 31,720

Celeste: May
Mystic Zodiac, Book 5

Celeste Kincaid is on a mission: Find the injured deer in the woods near her home and heal it. Once she does, she can get back to her *real* job; healing animals brought into her practice and teaching the next generation of faerie healers. She can also get back to dipping her toe in the dating scene. But from the onset of the task, she gets the feeling something isn›t right. When she finds the injured deer, which ends up being a sick fawn in the back yard of the sexiest Wood Elf she's ever seen, she knows something is up.

Owen Foster is in love, well, at least lust at first sight. The blonde-haired goddess standing in his backyard is every man's fantasy come true; until she opens her mouth and accuses him of being a crappy elf. He can overlook that misguided belief as he helps her care for the fawn, but when her youngest sister shows up and acts like they're together, he'll have to go to desperate measures to prove they aren't.

A meddling mother dabbling with faerie magic, the worst storm they've ever seen, along with a bear and a fawn — will these two be able to turn their instant attraction into a love of a lifetime?

Word Count: 32,915

About the Author

Brandy is a paranormal romance author who, on occasion, likes to dabble with contemporary. She's addicted to murder mystery shows and who-done-its. You'll almost never see her without some type of skull paraphernalia on and is always dreaming of more tattoos.

Brandy is a Navy brat, prior enlisted Army, current Army wife, and mom. She lives in Virginia with her husband of almost 20 years, their three kids and one dog.

Brandy is all over the web. Pick one or all to keep up with her.
Don't forget to sign up for the newsletter. There is a monthly giveaway and when the mood strikes other fun things like deep discounts in the shop.

Website | brandywalker.net
Facebook Author | facebook.com/BrandyWalkerfanpage

Books by Brandy Walker
TEZ PUBLISHING

Tiger Nip
Craving More, Book 1
Claiming More, Book 2
Dallas & Kacie: Tiger Bite, Book 2.5
Finding More, Book 3 (Aug/Sep 2015)
Giving More, Book 4 (TBD)
Seeing More, Book 5 (TBD)

Freefall
Caught in the Moment, Book 1
Fly Guy Next Door, Book 2
Captured by Color, Book 3 (TDB)
Revving Her Engine, Book 4 (TBD)
Spinning Out of Control, Book 5 (TBD)

Praetorian Guards
New series in the works

Keystone Predators
Under Her Spell
In the *Romancing the Wolf* Box Set

Stand Alone
Her Destiny
In the *Shifters Gone Alpha* Box Set

Mystic Zodiac
Thane | January | Angel
Parvati | February | God/Goddess
Gideon | March | Shifter

**B
O
N
U
S**

DECADENT PUBLISHING
ROAR LINE

Shifter U

21693577R00108

Made in the USA
Middletown, DE
08 July 2015